SWIFTS AND OTHER STORIES

Dominic O'Sullivan was born in North London and grew up in Muswell Hill. He has, however, spent much of his time in East Anglia. He studied German at the University of East Anglia under the guidance of his tutor Dr W G 'Max' Sebald.

He has taught English as a Foreign and Second language as well as French, German and Italian in a number of London Colleges and Universities. In addition to teaching he has been involved in translation work in both French and German.

This is his first collection of short stories and he has also had one play performed.

SWIFTS AND OTHER STORIES

D O'Sullivan

SWIFTS AND OTHER STORIES

Olympia Publishers

www.olympiapublishers.com
OLYMPIA PAPERBACK EDITION

Copyright © D O'Sullivan 2009

The right of D O'Sullivan to be identified as author of this work has been asserted in accordance with sections 77 and 78 of the Copyright, Designs and Patents Act 1988.

All Rights Reserved

No reproduction, copy or transmission of this publication may be made without written permission.
No paragraph of this publication may be reproduced, copied or transmitted save with the written permission of the publisher, or in accordance with the provisions of the Copyright Act 1956 (as amended).

Any person who does any unauthorized act in relation to this publication may be liable to criminal prosecution and civil claims for damage.

A CIP catalogue record for this title is available from the British Library.

ISBN: 978-1-905513-99-4

This is a work of fiction.
Names, characters, places and incidents originate from the writer's imagination. Any resemblance to actual persons, living or dead, is purely coincidental.

First Published in 2009

Olympia Publishers part of Ashwell Publishing Ltd
60 Cannon Street
London
EC4N 6NP

Printed in Great Britain

For Peter and Mary

In fond memory of Pamela, Terence, Kathleen and Fred.

Swifts

Where did I first meet them? Now, you've got me. Good question that. Let me think. That's right. It was during the long hot summer. Quite ironic then that it should prove so productive, but yes, it was during those endless weeks of drought.

I first saw them on the pier. I was walking round as you do and I saw her face under a ring of those coloured light bulbs. The sea roared and I could see the foam through the slats. It was slowly getting dark, but there was still the last of the sunset, which hadn't yet vanished behind the cliff.

They both looked very young, and so they were of course. Those eyes. Those pale blue eyes. They sparkled in the lights and I could hear laughter. In the distance the church tower loomed up, watching us, adding its blessing. Have you noticed how in that part of the country they go in for those tall church towers?

As they left the pier I followed, but whereas I walked along the esplanade, they abruptly turned right and up the steps. I remember the swifts screaming and flying low – the first real heralds of summer, as swallows are apt not to bother with some towns.

I sat and sipped my beer and said, "You're beautiful," for beyond the amber glass and the sighing, shifting sea, those eyes imprinted themselves on me, and I heard her laugh once again.

The next day the rain came; a sullen drizzle and a sea mist. The town as empty and deserted as if an unexploded bomb had drifted up on the beach.

But on the Saturday in the Life Boat Café – I believe, I really believe – fate struck. At the next table, there she sat.

Quick, I thought, say something, seize the moment, throw a line to a drowning man, but, "Could you pass the salt?" was all I said. The salt was in one of those big, heavy dispensers and wobbled manically across the table.

I passed it back. I couldn't ask for it again. She got up – going – although she'd left her coat. But no. False alarm. She went to the counter and ordered another tea.

The seagulls were flying out after the fishing boats. Have you noticed that herring gulls have a nasty laugh? That is, when they're not screeching wildly across the harbours.

She came back and then suddenly lurched forward. The table leg had tripped her up and sent a shower of tea in my direction.

"Oh, I'm so sorry," she said.

"No, no, it's okay, no damage done."

I hastily wiped the tea from my white flannels.

"It's these stupid legs."

"No problem."

She smiled in embarrassment. So tea had worked where salt had failed. We began to talk.

"We're going back on Friday. James works weekends."

"James?"

"My brother."

"Oh, what does he do?"

"In a hospital. Porter."

We talked and talked. The sea rattled the pebbles. Half an hour later, James arrived.

"What kept you?" she asked him.

"Left my sunglasses in the pub, didn't I?" he replied.

That evening I met Annie and James for a drink. The weather had returned to normal and we sat outside, quaffing pints as the tide began to turn, dragging across stones on the beach and buffeting the frail looking supports of the pier.

I looked into those beautiful eyes and was hypnotised.

By the end of the week, Anne's cheeks were glowing.

"The air's so fresh up here," she laughed.

"Nonsense, it's all that drinking. Honestly, she doesn't normally drink that much," quipped James.

I smiled. We swapped addresses. Little bits of precious paper. And this time no idle holiday exchange. I would write. We would meet up. I'd make sure of it. Definitely.

I kissed her goodbye on both cheeks and James squeezed my arm. They stepped into the truncated train and were gone. A last wave from the window. A puff of blue between rolling hills. It's not as flat as you think... silence. Solitude. I was back to being alone but it didn't bother me. I would definitely write.

Thereafter, the post cemented our union. Hesitantly at first. Little spidery writing. Amoebas crossing the page. Then more often. Come and see us. How about it?

A train riding over the low marshes of the east, swaying in the breezy emptiness. I nearly missed the station. Small and unapologetic, only two carriages contriving a match with the platform. A wooden hut for shelter, a ticket office long abandoned, and James leaning against it, grinning at my brief panic.

"I'm afraid she's stood you up. She's playing tennis so she sent me to pick you up. Some knockout tournament."

We walked up a reedy lane flanked by dykes and drains.

"Fancy a drink?" said James. "Celebrate your arrival."

As we sat outside the weather-boarded pub, I noticed how white his teeth were.

"This is why I didn't take the car. Excellent stuff," he said.

The beer was heady and hoppy, and I felt uncoordinated as we approached the house. Trees waved around the low, stone building, offering scant protection from the wind. I stayed a long weekend. Played tennis every day. Balls lobbing in a ballooning breeze. Canoed down the narrow river and was almost garrotted by overhanging branches. They tenderly extricated me from the advances of willow, brushing off the leaves and stray bits of bark.

I came back most weekends and was garrotted more. Anne came to London and so one day in late autumn, leaves still fluttering on trees, we tied the knot. Little café near Holborn Circus. Words nearly drowned by the espresso machine.

Anne rang to tell them at home, then made another call to tell

James. He was rambling in the Lake District. Buttermere. She had to tell him too. It was always like that. Instinctively thought about each other. Reflex action. Like mirror image twins – except they weren't. She returned beaming after making the calls. We went to a restaurant to celebrate. Groomed spinach accompanied by paltry potatoes and lamb resting forlornly on three leaves of cress. We should have stayed in the café and inflated ourselves with lasagne.

After a while we moved. Anne didn't like big cities so it was back to the countryside. It was all the same to me. More travelling but less hassle. We saw quite a bit of James.

At weekends, when Anne was doing her stained glass stuff, James and I cycled off to obscure pubs with unknown beers. Roads that always went upwards whichever way you went, and a biting wind that blew into you. Many a time we saved each other from lurking ditches as we missed the zigzags of the road.

But Anne put down her stained glass for our second anniversary and we went back to the coast.

"I'm not camping!" she protested. "No way."

In fact, the weather settled the argument. Grey skies and chilly winds buried the atmosphere of balmy evenings. The swifts had long gone, abandoning the summer, leaving the gulls to shriek across the harbour. I wondered whether Anne would want James to come but she made no mention.

We walked along the beaches most days, taking in the crisp sea air. One afternoon we went on a longer walk and headed beyond the pier. Those beautiful eyes, I thought. Long stretches of sand tapering into nowhere. Constant ripples in slate-grey sandpools. Looking out to sea, a mist was beginning to form, and there was the distant sound of a foghorn.

The pier was what started it, I thought to myself, as we kicked against unexpected pebbles and skirted around rockpools. I looked behind us, but there was nothing but open beach and waves crashing against breakwaters.

We went up to the cliffs. A kestrel was drifting above. The ground was still moist after the morning drizzle.

We trod paths that wound through bracken and gorse. I had no idea of the time, but Anne kept looking at her watch.

We turned back, Anne walking slightly ahead on the narrow path. Birds scuttled across, low-flying and scolding. The mist brooded on the horizon.

Even now I can't really recall it. You know, when your mind goes blank sometimes. But I do remember the foghorn. That bleak doleful sound.

Just at the bend in the cliff path Anne had slipped. It may have been the wet stones or sudden subsidence, although she was never that nimble on her feet.

Of course everyone was sympathetic… sometimes painfully so. But between those long staring silences I had James all to myself. He would be in need of comfort. Such beautiful eyes.

Hoodwinked

"Blimey, she's barmy," muttered Ron, as she staggered towards the taxi.

The hooded figure paused and gestured towards the suitcase.

"Lady, what you got in here? The kitchen sink?" Ron grumbled.

"No, the fridge," she replied tartly and gave her destination.

"I think it'll be shut, love."

"Don't you 'luv' me," she said by way of distraction, and got into the purring taxi.

It was getting dark; trees and shrubs paraded past the window.

"Are you sure you want to go there?" he repeated. "It'll definitely be shut."

Hilda took no notice. The rhythmic passing shrubs made her think of heady days in the shop. The early mornings, oh so early, drawing back the curtains and treading on dew-drenched lawns. Just before she passed through the gate, she loved to plunge her hands into the cool grass and watch the droplets trickle over her arms. As she walked the mile and a half to work, Hilda could picture Trevor bending over the oven. She loved his arse. Simply loved it. There was nothing better than when she casually nudged past, leaving floury handprints all over his neat blue-trousered bottom.

Time and again she did it, till he got narked.

"I kept getting funny stares all morning, Hilda, so cut it out."

She sniggered. He was so sweet and his eyes flashed when he got angry. Such lovely eyes.

"Excuse me for asking," enquired Ron, "but have you joined an order or do you normally dress up as a nun?"

Hilda gave a start and looked at the broad neck in the front of the cab. Not a patch on Trevor's bottom, she thought.

"Oh this? Well, we've been rehearsing and I simply didn't have time…"

Ron slowed down to approach a roundabout.

"And if you don't mind me asking, where do the roller skates come in?"

She clattered coyly and giggled.

"It's a variation on one of those Andrew Lloyd Rhubarb things. I have to circle round the stage singing 'The hills are alive…' I'm all equipped with flashing lights. It's going to be very visual."

"Must be," said Ron, who'd never made it further than the Cromer End of Pier show. And who was he to argue?

They passed down the long avenue which threaded through a housing estate. The battered bus shelters bore testimony to the fragile remains of the town bus service, the last remnant of which was seldom seen after seven o'clock.

She remembered the queues sometimes outside the bread shop, and Charlie who worked in the cash cubicle of the butcher's. It was more hygienic then, when they didn't mix meat with money.

"Here's the church," she exclaimed," Wait here!"

She skated under the drooping oak and negotiated the two or three steps up to the porch. In a moment or so she was whispering through the grill of the confessional, her soft, sibilant sounds like the twittering of morning sparrows.

The clock ticked round. A candle flickered.

"Bless me, Father, for what I am about to do…"

"I see." Father Joe listened. "Well, I concede you have a point, if a little drastic."

It was over. She left the confessional, shut the wooden gate and was out on the porch.

A passing builder made her think of Trevor, and she was back again in the shop. It was Christmas and bonhomie was in the air. No tinsel, as it tended to get tarnished with baking flour – but the heady smell of mulled wine… and after…

The toot of Ron's taxi disturbed her reverie. She scowled and skated towards the car.

"Some people don't know the meaning of patience," she grumbled. "It's me who's paying you!"

"I've got another job after this, lady," he remonstrated.

"Oh shut up!" she snapped. "And drive on!"

The spire of the church behind disappeared into darkness as they bobbed swiftly towards the ring road. Here was the smell of mustard factory mingled with the waft of beer from the one remaining brewery. They climbed the narrow bridge over the river, with the trees in the nearby park fading fast into twilight.

She sighed. Trevor and she had often lain under the bridge listening to the rain. Soggy crisps on wet afternoons. A pickled gherkin for Saturday night. A Walnut Whip on Wednesdays.

Life had not been without its little pleasures, and she drifted back to the shop again. It was Easter; time for the occasional chocolate departure from a rigid Bakewell routine.

They were getting nearer now; in fact, they were almost there.

Her sense of well-being gave way to nausea. There it was – awful in its enormity, like a kind of housing estate spread over the marshes. First of all came the lights of the petrol station, and then, in neo-lavatory style, the hybrid horror of the hypermarket.

She hated it. Hated it for everything. Not just for what it had done to High Streets up and down the country, but she also hated it for the eventual closure of Trevor's shop.

Of course he no longer worked there, but it had been a baker's up until the last six months, and now it lay empty and forlorn, coated with green and yellow stickers for Billy Graham and Bhagwan.

This was a double desecration of the shrine.

The cab circled a moment or two in the deserted car park.

"I told you, lady."

"Here," she said," help me with this case."

Hilda stumbled out of the cab and wobbled precariously with her suitcase. She staggered up to the huge glass doors of the hypermarket.

"'Ere lady," shouted Ron. "What you gonna do with...?"

Ron felt uneasy as the veiled Hilda bent over and undid the flaps. Within moments she had produced something looking rather like…

"A ruddy bomb!" shrieked Ron. "Crikey, she's mad. 'Ere, give me that!"

It was too late, for Hilda had swiftly triggered a device and was skating like mad past Ron towards the exit of the car park. She cackled gleefully, invisible now in the darkness. For good measure she smashed a giant burger sign to the left of the automatic car-wash.

Ron seemed to freeze for a moment. Then a blaring car horn from somewhere jolted him into action. He jumped back into his cab and drove off.

The camouflaged Hilda was nowhere to be seen as he drove frantically out of the car park, which was thanking him for his custom, and onto the main road.

Suddenly there was a loud rumble and the world was raining glass. The hypermarket was at least living up to its name, as parts of it orbited above the street lamps. Plastic seats from cash tills bounced furiously across the tarmac, while a thousand Angel Delights were now being reconstituted in the ornamental fishpond.

The following day, a taxi driver answering to the name of Ron, was apprehended. A write-up appeared that evening in the local paper. Ron's taxi had apparently been spotted by a distraught petrol pump attendant.

Apart from driving off at high speed, the taxi driver appeared to have been badly concussed following the explosion.

Mr. Ron Bassetwood keeps referring to a nun on roller skates singing 'The hills are alive…' and 'I did it for you Trevor'.

Ever Decreasing Circles

The image of the rippling pool abated. Gradually with time, and like the ripples themselves, they burst and broke upon the banks. Only grief hadn't quite receded. It was habitually present; a dull ache like a nagging tooth or a toe blister pressed against the shoe.

Leaves parted and he was hurtling through the undergrowth. Almost in slow motion, he could see the swaying branch. The pattern of shed leaves crunched on the floor under the urgent panic of his feet. Joe's cries for help had suddenly subsided. He was wading into the pond – dark, inky water that now bubbled evilly round his mouth. Then they were picking up that little shape, that sopping bundle, and screaming wildly across the conspiratorial silence.

Caroline was next to him, hysterical. Then everything became confused, waterlogged splashing. Breathing into his little mouth as he lay on the clay bank; futilely pumping his motionless chest; that terrible stillness.

The family in room 3 let out a shriek. The word 'cheat' resounded in chorus.

He and Caroline had lasted nine months after that, but the drifting away from each other had begun before Christmas. They were each a reminder to the other, and, in the ensuing numbness, were somehow unable to console one another. They saved their tears for empty rooms, as if the visible show of grief would infect each other.

They parted, wrote occasionally – postcard-type letters – token platitudes. Everything was so safe.

Then he met Eileen, and shortly after, Caroline wrote to tell him about Ian.

The backstreet bed and breakfast was in a small seaside town. Eileen had inherited it from her aunt, and somehow the fresh, salty air, the compact garden full of creeping nasturtiums, offered the change he needed. No nine to five. No spasmodic and overcrowded trains. Enough work with hotel and garden to keep him busy. And Eileen was so different. She was calm, methodical and seemed to understand him intuitively. When memory clouded his face, she pressed him against her shoulder and ran her long fingers softly against the back of his neck.

There was no pond in the garden, but stray frogs and toads hinted of a nearby presence. There was a greenhouse to which he retreated in the quieter winter months. In mid February or March, it housed a small paraffin heater, which glowed from the twilight hours to early morning.

As Easter beckoned, guests started to appear at the B&B. Streaky bacon smells wafted into the hall, and each morning he got up at six, leaving Eileen slumbering, to prepare the breakfasts.

There was one last shriek of 'cheat' and Miss Warburton was knocking at the door. It appeared her towel had gone missing again.

"Can't have that now, can we?" he said and led her to the linen cupboard.

This was another tranquil place, like the greenhouse. Various smells of comfort and pine combined with the smell of warm linen. A wholesome void, calm and still – no ripples.

When the Wilkinsons booked in on Friday evening, they were full – the first time that year.

"Looks like we're in for a busy summer," he said to Eileen that evening. "And the weather looks set to last."

She looked up from her book. "I shan't complain." Then with a smile, "You never know, we might make enough to go on holiday."

"Maybe," said Michael, unconvinced.

"Either that or look for a bigger place."

"Hmm," he grunted. "Sounds like more hard work. And that way we'd never get to take a holiday."

"Pessimist."

"Let's see how the summer goes," he said as he went to put the kettle on. As it chugged away, he wondered where they would go. Their first holiday.

"It's a bit early, I think," he said. "I don't know."

With the hotel full, he was getting up earlier to do the breakfasts. At half past five he stepped onto the dew-soaked lawn, the grass soft and cool between his open sandals. Water. Circles. He tried not to think. He went back to the kitchen and shut the door, quickly spearing a pack of bacon. The greenhouse glinted in the early sun. The only sound in the kitchen was the sudden murmuring of the fridge, followed by the chinking sound of milk bottles on the back doorstep.

Eileen had a headache that morning, so he told her to stay in bed. He'd be fine – yes. He could do it all – he'd manage.

By eleven thirty he was finished, washed up and all, and taking a mug of tea up to Eileen.

Suddenly his thoughts were interrupted by a soft tapping at the door. A girl and a boy stood in front of him.

"We can't get into the room. It's the door," the girl said.

She had a wide spread of freckles emanating from her nose, and with her red hair she looked like a spotty lion cub.

Michael accompanied them up the stairs.

"Everybody's out shopping," the girl said, "and we couldn't get in."

"Oh I see, yes. That door sometimes sticks. We'll get it fixed." He leant his shoulder hard against the door and it grudgingly gave.

"Try not to slam it too tight. We'll get it sorted later."

Two footsteps followed him as he turned back downstairs.

"What's in the glass house in the garden?" the boy asked.

"That's my greenhouse, where I grow the plants to put in the borders."

"Can I have a look?"

"Yes, of course. I'll just take this tea up and I'll see you down there in a moment. Don't go in, will you?"

"No."

The diminutive solitary figure had his back to him as he stepped out for the second time into the garden. The sun dazzled through the glass, glinting fiercely off the neat aluminium frame.

Michael slid back the door and they stepped into greenhouse heat. Spiders scuttled behind staging as they trod gingerly over the boards.

"There's sometimes a frog hidden under this plank of wood. Shall we see if he's still there?"

The boy nodded as Michael turned over the board. Squinting beneath the wood was a squat brown and yellow frog.

"Ohhh," said the boy, and slipped a hand into his.

He put the other hand out to touch the tiny frog, but Michael stopped him.

"We don't want to frighten him, do we?"

"No, we mustn't." The boy looked back at him and it was then, in the greenhouse of the sun, that Michael saw him clearly for the first time.

His mouth dropped open and he murmured the word, "Joe."

Joe's blue eyes looked back at him, that familiar studious and forlorn expression.

"Oh Joe," he whispered. "Joe."

He picked the boy up, that soft cheek caressing his line of stubble. Kissing him repeatedly, he held him tightly against his neck.

"At last," he said," at last we've found you. Mummy will be pleased. She'll be so pleased.

He didn't hear the child's frantic screams. All he saw was the bright, radiant sun as he bundled the boy into the car and drove off at full speed to tell Caroline.

At Night

There was a monster in the back bedroom, Damian thought, as he looked at the rain pouring across the garden. He'd heard it, hadn't he?

He snatched the battered Ford Capri and ran it along the window ledge, the neat suspension negotiating flaky paintwork. Inside, a diminutive driver sat motionless behind a huge steering wheel. Footsteps in the hall. His mother going, no doubt, to the freezer to get some more beefburgers. Rain dripping outside the window. The lawn fluorescent green and looking like the bathroom sponge. Damian liked it whenever he trod the path, listening to the water hiss up from the grass and trickle down the cracked patches of concrete.

But as for that monster, it definitely lived in the back room.

"You're going to the Garricks' after tea," said Marie, bumping a plate down in front of him.

Damian looked up at her with a disgusted stare.

"I don't want to."

"Tough," came the reply. Then to placate the inescapable stare, she added, "It's only for an hour," and ruffled his straw brown hair. "I can't really get someone to babysit for an hour, can I?"

He kept his eyes on her.

"Besides, Mrs. Garrick likes having you. She does. And I know Lucy isn't exactly your age, but she looks forward to seeing you too."

"It's so boring," said Damian, chewing his beefburger in a deliberately ugly fashion. He reached mutinously for the tomato ketchup, smiting the bottom of the bottle a few extra times for good nature.

A little while later, he was duly dropped outside the Garricks' home. As he walked the few steps up the path, he noticed the big Mercedes had disappeared from the drive. This was the one possible source of interest to him. It had buttons inside that made the mirrors move around. The aerial went up and down and then lowered like a periscope. He wasn't sure if it had a phone inside too, but it could splosh water quite dramatically over its windscreen like a persistent whale.

It was will sadness that he looked at the empty spot on the gravel path as the door swung open to meet him. Even worse, he was inside the house before he could press the bell that played a tune.

Damian looked around the hall. There seemed to be so many rooms leading off.

"Damian," cooed a voice. "Come on in."

He stood on springy carpets while Lucy watched him from the stairs.

"Perhaps you'd like to go up to Lucy's room today. We've got some visitors coming."

Mrs. Garrick propelled him in the direction of Lucy.

Lucy, tiny in her strawberry tights, was looking very smug for some reason. He followed the strawberry up the staircase. It was the first time he'd been in her room. As usual, toys formed an assault course on the floor, over which Mrs. Garrick would gingerly tread.

As Damian looked at a row of glass tanks by the window, Lucy, lip quivering and face beaming, said, "I've got a parrot." And there, sure enough, immobile yet alive, a beautiful green and yellow parrot stared quizzically at the new attendant. It had a red spot on its bill and its scarlet cheeks made it look as if it were permanently embarrassed.

Damian stopped to look at it; at the same time, his mouth dropped open.

"What's his name?" he asked.

"Well actually," said Lucy superciliously, "we don't know if it's a boy or a girl."

"Why not?"

"It's very difficult to tell when he's very young."

"So how do you know he's a he?" persisted Damian.

Lucy ignored him and stroked the yellow and green parrot.

"Buttons," said Lucy, "Mrs. Winch thought of Buttons."

Damian made a face.

"It's a stupid name," he said, but even so, he moved a hand forward gingerly to stroke the becalmed bird.

"Here's my doll's house," said Lucy after a while, seeing Damian might become too well acquainted with Buttons. "It was made for me specially."

Damian peered in through the various windows; the hall with its fitted radiators, the little study with its reading lamp. In the living room, figures sat in cosy armchairs round a log fire.

He watched mesmerised for a while. Everything was so calm and stable. The rooms with their leisurely figures seemed so permanent and still. Quite unlike...

Damian got up, rubbing a spot on his knee. Lucy's face required an answer.

"I like the parrot more," he said, determinedly. "You can stroke him."

Later, when Damian was brought home at about eight, he noticed that Uncle Larry had arrived. His black car was wet and gleaming in the drizzling rain. Damian told them all about the parrot, that he'd stroked it five, six, seven times – even though it was only twice, because, in truth, he was a little afraid of the bird with its sharp claws. They didn't seem very interested though.

"Time to go to bed." said his mother. "Say goodnight to Larry."

Damian went upstairs thinking of the parrot. He undressed and read his comic. Lying for a few minutes without any clothes on, on top of the covers, he could think of much better names than Buttons. Buttons. He said it out loud. Then he turned out the light and pulled the bedclothes round him.

The parrot nodded its head before his eyes, for Damian was now its proud owner. It had learnt to speak better than anybody else's. It was very tame and came onto his hand. It said lots of things and was particularly fond of sausages. At the school they were amazed. In the playground, a circle of admirers had gathered round, hands reaching out nervously and tentatively to touch it. Even better, the parrot pecked the hands of those it didn't like.

But at that moment Damian opened his eyes and the parrot disappeared. His bedroom stared back at him in darkness. It was raining again outside so that the water gurgled down the drainpipes and resounded off next door's dustbin lids.

The wind blew gently through the half open window; the window through which the parrot had escaped into the night air. The curtain fluttered and he shivered; he was now feeling a bit cold so he crept out of bed to close it. He tried not to bang the window or thump his feet on the floor. It was quite hard to shut as it had got stuck in the damp, but finally he managed to do it. The sound of muted rain could be heard outside.

Then, as he got back into bed, another sound. Damian stopped and listened. He listened carefully. The wind blew against the window, but he could still make the noise out.

There it was, without a doubt. The monster in the back room.

Turning the door handle gently, he slipped out into the passageway. He stopped. Maybe he should go back in. Forget all about it. Maybe it would eat him though. But then, if he was in bed, it could still come and eat him. That would be worse. And the parrot that could protect him had gone.

No. He'd have to let everyone know. Raise the alarm. So he inched forward into the darkness, hearing the sound again. The floorboards creaked as he moved nearer to the door. Then he heard a low gasp. He pressed his ear against the wood, but the noise wasn't coming from there.

Then suddenly another door opened. A man was in the passageway, his shadow coming towards him.

He heard his mother in the distance, shouting "Don't, don't!"

Then, anxious footsteps and Larry shouting "The little bastard! Spying on us!"

Larry's face was quite different. His arms were raining blows. From nearby and yet a long way off, his mother screeched. As Damian felt the full impact of the onslaught, he screamed and shut his eyes. The parrot had gone.

Not Drowning But...

"I'm sure," said Sheila, "...in time."

"No," Bridy said and shook her head.

Her eyes came to rest on the black and white swirls of the ball, taking pride of place, as Dave would have it, on the gloomy sideboard.

Sheila caught Bridy's line of vision. "Another cup of tea perhaps? Shall I make it?"

"No," answered Bridy.

The ball billowed like a giant squid on the lonely dresser. It was barely a year old, but now it festered like an unloving mushroom of remembrance.

Two days ago, they had done it. Decided. In an hour of incessant rain that scattered shoppers from the pavements. The heavens wept their choked tears – collective, but mainly his. Even the car wouldn't start – they sat there watching the wipers flick across the blurred screen. And, as he thought afterwards, it was somehow grimly symbolic.

"Mum!" He was tugging at her elbow. "I'm in!"

"Sure, that's great news," she'd said without enthusiasm.

He picked up on it. "But I'm in."

She stopped what she was doing and threw him a brief smile. "I suppose there'll be more trips. Bound to be."

He went over and stuck a hand in the biscuit tin; a large, crumbly digestive, which sent a shower of biscuit fragments over the floor.

Bridy sighed. She had always resented him. Resented him ever since his unwarranted intrusion into the world. That night on

Hadleigh Common had been the night of his conception. Too much wine and an inadequate picnic hamper. The stars had been so clear; the air fresh and heady with the scent of pine. She and David had spent one blissful night together, until the early hours, then cycled precariously home for him to start the morning shift.

Daniel was on his way. Perhaps even then she knew he was destined to be a footballer by the ferocious kicking she'd had to endure. Easing her way back into work after a lengthy spell away had proved difficult. He'd spoilt that for her too. Then, of course, any social life went out the window. Fled, as if it were a bird on the wing. And she knew too, that some of her friends were avoiding her.

For the first few years he'd squawked like a voracious gull. He'd not been an amenable child. Then both of them seemed to disappear from her sights, as David said Daniel showed all the makings of being a footballer. They would vanish for hours on the common. Hours. Kicking a ball no doubt, across the site of his conception. Then Daniel became old enough to go to matches. Weekends saw her watering solitary rose bushes, somehow a frail symbol of her own isolation. To give her something to do, she had the patio uprooted and stocked it with extra plants.

David had remonstrated, "But there's nowhere for the lad to play."

She snarled at him. "He can use the park. Anyway, I'm not having him break my pots with that incessant thudding."

Slowly, they seemed to drift away as if relentless currents propelled them both in other directions.

"Are you sure there's nothing you want?"
Bridy looked blankly back. "What do I want?"
"From the shops," Sheila said.
Bridy shook her head. There was a long silence. The ball swivelled. It was mesmeric. It was as if the whole house was encapsulated in this one ball. The ball. Pride of place. How could she feel proud... ever?

"Dad, I'm in."

"That's great." And he lifted Daniel up and gave him a great big hug. He never hugged her like he hugged him. Either of them. It was as if Daniel knew he should instinctively shy away from her; from the tell-tale signs of smouldering resentment.

"Can we go out on the common?"

"Sure. What time's tea?"

"Six thirty," she lied, bringing it forward by nearly an hour.

"There's just time then. Let's take the bikes."

The front door slammed shut and in the ensuing silence she pressed the remote control to the opening theme of an evening soap.

It was getting dark. They were late. Time slipped by on the common, as well she knew, like nowhere else. They would be apologetic. There would be an atmosphere, and she'd be bribed with a 'put your feet up', while the kitchen would chink and clang to the sounds of their ponderous washing-up and endless football banter. She was the lodger who cooked the meals. It was nice of them not to ask for any rent.

"It's great that he's in the team.' David said to her in bed that night. "Really great."

She nodded as he held her tight. The last words she remembered him saying before falling asleep were "Oh, it's been a long day."

Of course they'd got him new kit and boots. The match was that Saturday.

"You are coming, love, aren't you?"

She wasn't sure. "I did say to…"

"He'd be so disappointed. Just this once." Something in his tone made it impossible to refuse. She'd postpone her visit to the garden centre in her quest for a suitable climber.

Daniel changed at home. He'd wanted to be seen by the neighbours getting into the car. He walked down the street three times to post letters and drew compliments. The red uniform enhanced his dark hair. He looked a bit like David when he was younger. The same dimpled chin. He looked grand.

They were driving to the ground against a background of non-stop chatter.

"Save your energy for the game," she'd told him. "You'll be worn out."

"The lad's excited," David said. "Looks great, doesn't he?"

The windswept field was full of little groups of mums and dads. The sky was overcast, grudging. Her mood mirrored the sky. Lombardy poplars swayed at the far end, while lorries chugged into the hangars of the recycling centre. It was a soulless ground, she thought, but then this was not a time for thinking. The game had already started. Spectators bellowing advice; cajoling, pleading, screaming.

She was wondering why the climbing rose was called Rambling Rector, whether it was because of excessive wordiness, when the cry went up. It was a solitary cry and the man next to her gave a gasp. David was out on the pitch. A small crowd had gathered round.

"What's happened?" she found herself asking, then realised, by looking at the other boys, that it was Daniel. Her legs were secured by heavy weights. Clouds flew overhead. She couldn't move. David was leaning over replica David and she heard the word ambulance.

She couldn't remember how long she stood there. There were people round her and someone was saying something to her, the mouth opening and closing like a fish in a tiny bowl. The siren jolted her back into action. She and David were in the ambulance. David kept stroking Daniel's forehead saying, "It'll be all right."

They bumped over endless speed humps. The hospital swallowed them up; endless corridors, white coats. White everywhere. White – the colour of amnesia.

He wasn't all right. Wasn't going to be. A kick to the side of the head. Complications. David explained it all to her after as she clenched the mug of lukewarm tea. The only thing they could do was go in each day and talk to him. David got time off work. Indefinitely. No, she didn't have to go in every day if she didn't want to. So long as someone was there.

The room became a little shrine. All it lacked were the candles. Scarves and banners draped around the bed. Football programmes in among the get-well cards. It went on for days, weeks, months.

One day, they had a special meeting with the consultant. "It was," he said, "for them... for them to decide." Switch off. Disconnect. Unplug a life.

David buried his head in her. "I can't bear it," he said, "to see him like this. I can't bear..."

"I know," she said, and ran her hand through his hair.

That evening he decided. The drifts of rain. She nodded. Whatever he wanted. She wanted whatever he...

When Ralph came to take them to the hospital, it was a light, sunny morning. They weren't fit, either of them, to drive. They could put Daniel's things in Ralph's car. It was big enough. He'd make a second journey if necessary.

"No," David said. They'd sort out his things, give the others away.

A bright and sunny day. They sat in the back, Ralph's bald patch making him look like a proper chauffeur, only he'd be wearing a cap if he were. Ralph talked about the changeable weather, nearly mentioned Everton; changed tack.

There was a new receptionist on the hospital desk, she noticed, as they took their familiar walk. They started counting down the rooms till they came to D16. Sixteen. It never came to that.

David and Ralph were taking away bits and pieces. The room was sunlit and the curtain fluttered in the breeze. She was left alone with her silent son. She glanced up at the rows of cards. Sometimes she tried to count them. There was a humming in the corridor. A vacuum cleaner; an electric wheelchair perhaps. It was while she was listening to the sound...

Suddenly a hand reached up and grabbed her. His hand. His. For a moment she didn't know what it was and screamed. The room went whiter still, turning inwards. She knocked over a vase.

David and Ralph ran quickly back, but all they could see was blood pouring from her arm and the broken fragments of glass. In an instant, the nurses were attending to her; stop the bleeding – words calming. She felt like she did on the football field when nothing in her moved. As the needle slid into her arm, she heard David saying to the nurse, "She's had a terrible ordeal... Only knows..."

The next morning they asked her if she wanted to go home. The curtains and the bandaged arm told her she was not at home.

"Daniel?" she asked David. "Daniel?"

"No," said David. "It's all over now. He's safe. He's where... Nothing's hurting him. They switched it off."

She drew herself up. "No!" she cried. "No! They can't have! No..."

As Sheila put down her cup and got up to go, Bridy remembered her words.

"In time. It'll all be behind you. You'll see."

"No," she screamed again. "Never!"

A Welcome Occupation

George Knebworth pulled back the curtains on another day. Behind the secondary, and in his view entirely unnecessary defence of net curtain, the morning was beginning to take shape.

Mavis stirred beneath the sheets. In another few minutes she would be fully awake, so George hurried with his dressing and went downstairs.

In the guests' dining room the smell of marmalade lingered in the air. In films of opium dens and seaside bars, large clouds of smoke and sin always hovered above the players. But in movies where Bed and Breakfasts appeared, they were unable to highlight the aura of marmalade.

He drew back the breakfast room curtains, casting an eye on the geraniums outside. Abandoning these thoughts, he placed the menus upright on eight likely tables, wiping away traces of egg with a damp cloth.

This was a pleasant time of the morning, a quiet time. No Mavis, no guests, no one, free. He fluttered like a bird into the kitchen and punctured the grapefruit can for Mrs. Armstrong. Pineapple would never do. It had to be grapefruit to perpetuate that sour expression. Even lemon juice couldn't extend the permanently dour features, the mouth forming a semi-circle of irreversible pessimism. As a nurse too, it was worse whenever she spoke. If ever there was any illness about, there was always some handy anecdote or prediction to make the victim feel worse and bring a hush to the breakfast room.

Mavis was coming downstairs. Only Mavis made the bottom stair squeak like that. It was the fanfare of the breakfast table. Oven and frying pan awaited her attention. Chilled bacon lay spread-eagled in the fridge and George diligently set to pouring out golden cereal into the glass bowls. The milk was fetched in from the crates outside and he ran his finger gently over the silver top, caressingly cool and reassuring as he dug his thumb into the tight seal.

"We've got more people coming this afternoon," Mavis announced from behind the kitchen hatch. "Then we'll be full. Germans, I think they are."

"Oh," said George, puncturing the second milk bottle, and he thought despairingly back to the Frau and Doktor Leibnitz they had had last autumn. Herr Leibnitz had complained afterwards to the Tourist Board because he, George, had omitted to remove a sock from the room belonging to the previous guests. Mavis had never forgotten that, never forgotten the stigma of the return letter from the Southsea Tourist Board. George had had to compose the contrite apology while Mavis thumped meal after meal down onto the table. He'd had to look assiduously under beds for weeks after. Then there had been Herr Doktor's circulation problems. It had all been too much.

"Then we'll be full," repeated Mavis.

"Yes, dear. I heard, actually."

"Heaven knows we need the money." Mavis was looking like a Lay Preacher.

"Oh come now," he said. "It hasn't been too bad a month really."

His reply was drowned by the rattling of china and Mavis setting the clock to the time signal.

At three o'clock, George was jolted from his siesta by a sharp ringing of the doorbell. Where was he? Breakfast. Yes. He hadn't... but no. Had he forgotten? They were expecting new arrivals.

He ran into the small reception room and looked at the book. Blast! He hadn't got his glasses and couldn't read the names. As a consolation, he thought he probably wouldn't be able to read them anyway. He flung open the door before it rang again and could summon Mavis. He was always nervous in front of guests when he was being watched. Always.

But instead of being confronted by Leibnitz the second, he saw the blurred images of two young girls standing at the doorstep.

"Good af-ternoon." The girls greeted him in hesitant English.

He took the outstretched hand offered to him.

"We are Inge und Mechthild Dolmetsch."

He was shaking hands with Inge now, or was it Mechthild?

"Oh, please come in," he said.

"Sanks."

"And what did you say your names were?"

"Bitte? Ah. Inge und Mechthild Dol…"

The book was still blurred to confirm any of this, but it seemed to bear out what they were saying.

"And how long will you be staying?" he asked them.

"We don't know. Maybe if it's a nice weather we stay one week."

"Fine." he said, pleased, and led them upstairs.

He showed them into the little twin room overlooking the bay and the front garden full of geraniums.

"There's no hot water in the room, but there's a bathroom across the landing." He pointed.

"Sanks," they both said.

"Thank you," said George, trying to remember his one word of German.

He went back to the hotel reception a transformed man. Even without his glasses, the new apparitions appeared like angels, particularly the fair-haired one, whom he called Brunnhilda. He watered the plants in the hall and tidied up his desk.

Already the angel was back.

"Which time is za brekworst?"

"Oh," said George, "from quarter to eight until nine o'clock." He mimed circles on an imaginary watch.

"And can my sister hev a bold egg? She always has a bold egg. It's so good for her digestion."

"Certainly." said George. "Of course. Danke." It had come back to him.

"Oh," said the angel, obliged to acknowledge. "Where ditch you learn your German?"

"Nowhere really," said George tongue-tied. "Just the odd word."

For the next two days it seemed a breath of fresh air had descended upon the guest house. The girls always had their breakfast at the last possible minute. Was it because they could claim his attention for themselves, he wondered, when all the other guests and matronly matrons had eaten at their appointed hours?

Mavis hadn't been too pleased about the egg. It was only for Fridays, she said, and George had no right to promise it, but George brought it out to Brunnhilda's younger sister in a specially polished egg-cup. The next morning she even asked for an extra egg.

Routine at Sunningdale Croft became punctuated in the most exquisite way. Brunnhilda asked. Brunnhilda got. Brunnhilda's spotted underwear took pride of place on the clothes line.

On the tiny balcony, Brunnhilda's towels flapped like pink flags of a welcome occupation. And when Brunnhilda's drying drawers fell by chance into the azalea bush, George rescued them with such care that even Mrs. Mint the cleaner, lowering her duster, couldn't help but notice.

George got up even earlier now to start the day. He was up an hour after sunrise, inhaling the smell of dew on the small square of lawn, his thoughts broken only by the clanking of milk crates. Summer seemed finally to have arrived. Strange how he'd never noticed it before.

Then it finally happened. Brunnhilda and her slightly darker sister were proffering outstretched hands. No, this wasn't the usual ritual before breakfast, when George came to deliver the boiled egg. They were dressed in raincoats now and had travelling bags at their feet.

George hadn't seen Brunnhilda so heavily dressed for some while. He hung onto her small hand for a moment or two.

"We go now." Brunnhilda said. "The weather is bad and we have a cousin in Canterbury."

Inge smiled.

"Well, you'll come again I hope." George said. "It's been very nice to have you. You know, bit of a change."

"Oh sure," Brunnhilda said, tossing her long hair back and looking at her sister. "We come back."

George accepted Inge's outstretched hand and then they made their way down the path. A sudden burst of sun lit up the sea behind the funereal taxi.

"Goodbye," said George from the breakfast room window, when the taxi had swung out of sight.

"What?" said Mavis as she took the last few plates and eggcup to disappear into the washing-up bowl. "What did you say?"

"Nothing." said George in reply. "Just…"

A few bubbles gurgled up from the eggcup.

"We'll have to think about selling up if it doesn't get a move on," said Mavis, arms working furiously.

But George in deafness, reached for the tea towel.

Stepping Out

His skin was pale under the shade of the green garden umbrella. Earlier she'd paid him a compliment as he was downing the last of his lemon barley.

"You still look young for your age," she said.

He smiled, noticing something in the bottom of the glass, and squeezed her hand. She turned away from her contemplation of shrubs.

"I'm worried about Gary," she murmured. "Do you think it'll do him good?"

"Course it will," Gerald said. "It's the gradual weaning process from home. Learn a bit of independence." He sighed. "Who knows, we might even get appreciated."

Annette put down her glass. "This water tastes funny," she replied. "What do they put in it?"

He shrugged. "I never drink it on its own. That's why."

She had her argumentative face on. "Couldn't your lot do something about it? Clean up their standards? Heaven knows we pay enough for it. And look at all those people in Cornwall nearly poisoned! All the company got was a measly fine."

Gerald smiled. Annette always referred to his lot as 'your lot'. From day one, they had never agreed on politics.

"Have a word with the Minister. Fine them. Renationalise them. I can't take to drinking lemon barley."

The earth was dry and dusty in the garden. The rhubarb had gone to seed, she noticed, sending out big frothy plumes above its slightly shrivelled leaves.

"That pig ate rhubarb in the film last night. What was it called?"

"The pig? I didn't see it."

"No, the film." After a pause she carried on, "I suppose the good thing is that Gary might make some new friends. He spends far too much time in front of that computer."

And indeed, as she looked up, she could see a head bent in the upstairs window to confirm what she had just said. "It's a crime to be in on a day like this. So beautiful…"

"Sorry, darling, I didn't hear. What's a crime?"

Annette threw him an exasperated look. "I suppose that's why you're in politics," she said. "The inability to listen."

"I'll make you a Pimm's," he offered, "and then take Coco."

She lay back in the chair. The sun was starting to disappear behind the rooftops opposite. The bowed head upstairs stood up, then sat down again. She would do some work when he was out, do some reports, but not now as the sun was still pleasantly warm and drowsy.

Gerald was looking for Coco, dangling the lead as bait. Annette smiled. It was amazing how daft even the most worldly-wise could appear when serenading their dogs. She heard the gate shut. The garden was still.

Gerald walked down the avenue, looking at the peeling bark of plane trees, a sniffing hyena tearing at the lead in front of him. He cut through the maze of neat back streets, then over the bridge to the station. The new-liveried train emerged in a few moments, a touch self-consciously, he thought, and he stepped alone into the front carriage.

A voice from Radio 3 announced a plethora of stations, but the next one would do. He enjoyed short train journeys, and in eight minutes he found himself alighting at the deserted station. It was a dismal affair, a stone hut harbouring a two-slatted seat next to a flaking timetable, none of which really bothered him.

He wondered if Annette knew of his route, whether anyone had said to her that they had seen her husband and a dog boarding a train. But then they were hardly likely to, for like most inhabitants of Baltimore Avenue, they lived lives of splendid seclusion. And he was one of the faceless ones, wasn't he? Seldom seen, seldom heard, but adequate for the needs of the constituency.

The road he turned into now was a dead end, at the end of which was a mound and the beginning of woodland. He was still young for his age, he mused, in spite of... in spite of everything. It wouldn't make any difference if Gary came or went, but if the youngest, Tom...

Coco was pulling hard at the lead and looking to perform acrobatics on the ground. The harsh, rubbery smell of fox piss was all around. This would do, he decided. Leaving Coco to the delectation of senses, he wound the lead swiftly round the tree and tied it.

"Good dog," he said, walking slowly away from him.

Coco lowered his nose to the ground as one well heeled to a ritual. In the early days, he had scuppered everything with his incessant barking. Subsequent deprivations of privilege and admonitions had caused Coco to think again.

A few strides uphill took him to the top of a mount, where he could survey all around him. For such a fine evening it appeared strangely deserted. Gerald wondered why that was. Perhaps there was football on the telly again, a curse even in the best of summer months, but no, he couldn't recall any.

Suddenly, to the right, he could hear twigs breaking, and a little way off, he could see a white-haired figure with a potbelly. Gerald tutted inwardly. He was often here, roaming, the unofficial guardian of the blasted heath. The potbelly glanced around for a few moments, then walked slowly in the direction of the pond to ensconce himself on a neighbouring bench. He was sweeping, eyes sweeping. Gerald could hear a footfall behind him.

Behind a straggly line of hawthorn, he caught a flash of blue and white. He watched more closely, then started to follow. The hair was dark, the figure lithe and slim. This was altogether more promising, he thought and quickened his pursuit. The early evening walker vanished from view, then turned full circle, so that he came face to face unexpectedly with Gerald.

He was not disappointed. For a moment he seemed to fall into those dark eyes in appreciation, sensing too that the boy was a nice, comfortable height. His heart was beating quicker as the boy coolly and unflinchingly returned his gaze with the semblance of a smile. Then came the well-worn ritual, the bogus, aimless walk, ending in the seclusion of a bank of ivy that obscured them both from view. Gerald walked straight towards that smile and put his arms around him.

It was the best ever, it seemed to him later, as he laid his head appreciatively on the boy's shoulder to recover.

"Where are you from?" he asked him.

The first fragment of dialogue.

"Purley," said the boy, doing up his trousers. "And you?"

"Kingston," lied Gerald.

The boy tucked in his shirt and tightened his belt. "I used to go to college there."

"Oh," said Gerald, affecting interest, but concentrating more on the near perfect orb of the boy's left cheek. "What's your name, by the way?"

"Kevin," he replied.

"James," he lied, extending an incongruous hand. Then, after a silence, "Do you come here much?"

"I come plenty," the boy grinned, "but no, not that often. Just depends on the weather. If it's a nice afternoon…"

After a lengthy pause, Gerald said, "It'd be nice to meet again. Have you got a phone number I can reach you on?"

Kevin scribbled something hastily on a piece of card, then handed it to him.

"I'll ring you," said Gerald, but Kevin was already making his retreat through the bushes. He raised a hand in farewell salutation.

For a while Gerald stood listening to the sounds and smells of the wood, then made one last trip to the top of the mound. There were no early evening walkers, and the sun was beginning to dip behind the far line of trees. Casting a final glimpse at the view, he turned back to retrieve Coco.

It took him five minutes to return to the spot, but when he got there it was with a sense of bewilderment. Coco was nowhere to be seen. Gerald looked again at the tree Coco had been tied to, then checked if he was on the right path. After getting his bearings right, he realised he was. There was even a mat of squashed grass where Coco's tummy had patiently waited and in all probability slept. But now...

Panic began to seize Gerald and he shouted urgent yells of "Coco, Coco!" He had never run off before, and if he had, would have made his way back no doubt, to find Gerald with his hands full of Kevin. Then a worse thought dawned on him. What was he going to tell Annette and the others? And how come he had gone off to a woodland spot seven miles away without telling her? The wood clouded over with uncertainty, which calls of "Coco" only served to reinforce rather than dispel.

Had Coco done this on purpose to show him up? The one occasion he had really enjoyed himself, really had a good time, and then this had to happen. But what if Coco had been helped? It couldn't have been Kevin, because in all likelihood he didn't know about the dog. Or did he? Perhaps it was Potbelly! The ever pervasive Potbelly. And maybe too he had seen behind the ivy-screen, and it was a case of sour grapes.

"Coco! Coco! Coco!" he yelled.

In the unresponsive silence, the woodland yielded nothing. He began to walk the various paths swiftly, cursing Potbelly, Potbelly the prime suspect. How was he going to explain this? "Coco! Coco! Coco!"

Beyond the favoured rambling spot, the woods and heathland spread out for three or four miles more. Coco could be anywhere.

He rubbed the back of his neck in agitation. What was he going to do? What was he going to tell them? Why was there nobody around, just when you wanted them? Some days it was as overcrowded as a guppy tank, but now... just empty woodland and the light was beginning to go.

He sat down for a second on a solitary bench to gather his thoughts, and felt something dig him in his back pocket. Fumbling for a moment, he pulled out a piece of card. On it was the word Kevin and a telephone number. It jogged his memory – but now was not the time to think back to their brief encounter.

He stared at it again, then got up from the bench. It was a bit of a long shot but it might be worth it.

With a few parting "Cocos," he made his way out of the woods and back to the direction of the railway station. On the corner of Shelduck Avenue, and still in its original red livery, was the obliging oblong of a phone box. Reaching in his pocket for coins, he spread them out above the phone, then dialled Kevin's number.

A woman's voice answered, framed against a backdrop of squawking TV.

"I don't think 'e's back yet," she said, "but 'e's comin' back for 'is tea, I'm sure."

"Okay, thanks," he muttered.

The phone box became an enclave of gloom. The next call would have to be...

"Hang on," she called suddenly. "I think I can 'ear a key."

There was a long interval of suspense, during which Gerald inserted another coin. Then suddenly a rasping voice was in his ear.

"Yes?"

"Kevin? Kevin, this is Gerald."

"Who?"

"We met in the woods a while back."

For a moment the phone went muffled and he could hear a voice saying, "I'm going to take this upstairs."

For a further minute Gerald shuffled in the cubicle of uncertainty, until the phone was picked up again. With no TV for accompaniment, Kevin's voice sounded clearer but more mocking.

"Who did you say you were?"

"Ger-ald. We met at the... you know where."

"Sorry, mate. I think there's been some mistake. I met a geezer called James."

In a flash, Gerald realised his mistake. He had been undone by his customary duplicity.

"And who did you want to speak to?"

"Kevin," said Gerald, almost pleading with him. "You. Kevin."

"I think you've made another mistake," the voice said.

"But I…"

As the receiver went down on him, only to be followed by the engaged tone on his subsequent dialling, Gerald had heard another confusing noise.

At the same time that the voice had said 'mistake', he was sure, in the background, just very slightly, he had heard a solitary, mischievous and yet familiar bark.

Snowflakes

The plane touched down to muddled emotions. Emotions as scrambled as the raindrops on the taxi windscreen. What a flat place it was! Over fifty years!

Before the journey she had packed and re-packed the suitcase, pushing down the springy jumpers. But each time they bobbed back and snagged on the zip. They refused to lie down, so she flung the heavy dictionary on top of them, transferring the documents more prudently to her hand luggage.

"Are you sure you wouldn't like me to go with you?" Bernie had offered.

But Hannah shook her head. "You'd hate it. Be bored senseless."

A myriad of deflections, excuses.

"How do you know?" he started, but Hannah's expressionless face confirmed her resolve.

"You can always ring me," he said. "And I'll be over... in a flash." He grinned.

Sitting in the taxi it was better to be alone – it was as if no other conversations existed than those of functions. It was not a social trip at all, and her grasp of the language – the language she had grown up with – was now like stepping precariously on a highly polished floor.

"Here is the hotel."

The car that was poisoning half a bus queue had drawn up to a square fifties-style building. The word slab and slob combined as the taxi driver sat motionless, enthroned on his leather plinth and let her stagger out on to the rain drenched steps.

"Why am I doing this?" she asked herself, as banknotes were

passed to the driver's outstretched hand, and she whirled her way through the hotel's revolving door. In the hotel lobby a young girl mirrored her mother's face. She remembered, and was reminded why.

'Remembered' seemed such an inappropriate word she reflected later, sipping an evening brandy in the hotel's closing dining room.

Everywhere, long, drab net curtains – to keep everything out. Night, day, everything except memory, which fluttered back in under the long shrouds in the cocooned reception and lounge.

"If you want me over, just ring." Bernie's genial voice and grin. But this was no place for Bernie. His good humour and sense of fun was not for here. And tomorrow it would begin in earnest.

"Night honey," she could hear him say, as she stepped onto the balcony, looking at the lights of the fading, twinkling city.

In the fridge's mini-bar, the can of tonic had a dent in it. She decided against it, returning it to its lonely compartment. Pressing the light switch above the bed, she could hear the murmur of traffic from the street below. The room was still light from the street lamps and there was a loud whining coming from the fridge. It would be difficult to sleep at night, but even so, her body felt like a sack of potatoes.

The winter covered everything, a vast landscape of snow, she remembered, and that morning the first few flakes tumbled from the skies, a presage of the hard winter that flew in from the east.

'Nothing good ever comes in from the east', her taxi driver had said that morning, as he drove her towards the town hall.

"Not much better from the west either," she thought, but this remained voiceless, constrained by the lack of sleep and voids in the accompanying language.

On the way through the long unending boulevards and grey slab buildings, she tried to remember words. Some slipped like little fish through the net, while others remained cumbersome and immovable like seaweed.

"Here we are," said the driver. Hannah alighted and paid him, then walked swiftly up the steps. She was diverted into various offices, went up and down the main staircase, along bleached corridors. At last she stood before the translucent door.

They couldn't quite comprehend why she was there, and they lost patience a little with her halting speech, but eventually they gave her the information she needed. Before going to the land registry she would need a solicitor, and so she collected one who would also have the dual purpose of speaking the necessary language.

Bernie would be mowing the lawn, she thought, adding to the suburban chaos of machines, sitting down in his fold-up chair, pouring himself a bourbon. She could do with one too, but now her solicitor would have to be her only prop. Martin, tall, bespectacled and possibly a little hostile. Why had she come? Wasn't it better to…?

She put on her glasses as they surveyed the swathes of maps.

"I just want to know," she said, "you see?" as he looked at her, devoid of expression, but nonetheless polite, attentive.

"Do many people come back to see what happened?"

"I don't think so," replied Martin. "It is too complicated, especially when SRL is involved."

"SRL?"

"Land requisitioned by State. If that is so and some State building is on it, then it is difficult, well, almost impossible."

"And private?"

"Private, well, different, and if there is a case, of course you can claim."

They were driving out of the city into falling flakes, which now settled on the trees and scant hedgerows.

"In England," she said, "there were a lot of those, I remember. What is the word for them?"

Martin obliged.

"But not where I live now," she added.

The snow was settling, making a featureless landscape invisible. They were back in a small town, following a number 9 tram newly plastered in adverts.

"This must be a new thing," she said, pointing to the lurid letters of the cigarette makers.

"Yes," said Martin.

"A new kind of colonialism."

Martin did not return her wry smile, but looked puzzled, defensive. They stopped in front of a block of flats, where three sets of footprints had exited from the doorway. Again they consulted the map.

"Here is the railway," said Hannah, "then this must be the timber yard." Martin nodded in agreement.

"So this here is my grandfather's land, then?"

"Yes, yes."

"And this new building is also on the land?"

Martin followed the line her finger made.

"So that means I own this land now?"

He paused as if finally making sure. "Yes, yes, you do."

She was tired that evening when she returned to the hotel. She was the only person eating in the faded dining room, and she could see the staff were eager to go home. The cabbage was lukewarm, the waitress disinterested. She hadn't the energy to complain, something she knew Bernie would berate her for. She drank a vodka to chase away the cold that had penetrated into her, and walked the dimly-lit staircase to bed.

"I'm afraid," she said to herself in the darkened room. "Bernie, I'm afraid." She went to the window, looking down at the bobbing lights of trams, the rows of chimneys belching smoke... and for a moment they reminded her...

She shuddered. She could have done with another 'little water' – a vodka. She could feel the dry, biting wind penetrating through the fallen putty of the window. In America they never had winds like this – such cold. She was enveloped in the icy wind of recollection, and a lump seemed to bobble from her stomach into her throat, half-strangling her.

Martin was at the hotel promptly at half past eight. He helped her down the steps, half swept with fallen slushy snow, and into the immaculate car.

"I have to do this," she said to herself. They were both silent for most of the journey.

As they came nearer to their last stop she asked, "What do they think about people coming back to claim their property?"

Martin paused for a moment as if memorising or rehearsing a speech. He scratched his nose as they waited behind a bus. "People here think, well... maybe it's strange after such a long time. And as you know, it is a difficult problem. It is not easy."

They drove for miles across white, treeless country. The wind buffeted the sides of the car. Hannah began to feel a sickly chill come over her as the road sign announced they were nearly there. It seemed so normal, traffic lights, bread shop on the corner, pedestrian crossing. Why was she doing this? She could order him to turn round now and go back. Maybe this was the easiest solution. But the other Hannah, the one of reason, propelled her on. Not to know, not knowing, not ever knowing, would be far worse, of course. It was not much of a choice as they stopped opposite a garage.

"This is it?" she asked.

Martin nodded, and again they both consulted the map. Two coaches passed them and then a third. The word Oświęcim was unfurling and unfolding in her head. They looked at the flimsy map then straight ahead at the preserved horror entrance, as they both tried to get their bearings. As she looked down at the squiggly lines and squares her vision blurred, but she stared again, kept on looking.

"The boundary," she said. They traced it with their fingers.

"My grandfather's land then, too?"

"Here is the end," Martin pointed.

Silence. They both sat for a moment.

And then she knew. It was what her mother, the only survivor from her family, had kept all the time from her. Never wanted her to know.

She saw a party of schoolchildren alight from the coach. The teacher clapped his hands and vaguely, haphazardly, they gathered into a line.

"It was built on some of our land, then?" she said to him, and clasped her cheeks in horror.

Martin looked again; methodical, thoughtful. "It would seem so. Yes," he nodded.

She paused for breath. "What a terrible irony... terrible..." were her last words that seemed to fade into the air.

They sat in silence for a while, watching children playing, running beyond the fence.

Martin turned the car round. He would be responsible for any necessary paperwork, for carrying out her decisions.

Snow was falling in ever thicker flakes across the windscreen.

Undercover

The room is still and silent. It is the room of a dream, a dream that comes back time and again to haunt me, with increasing regularity. Into this room, slowly, comes a hand, a pair of hands, milky-white and soft. Gentle hands – but these hands, I'm bound to tell you, are going to cause a revolution.

I look at Rory, spooning cornflakes – milk flying off the swiftly raised kitchen implement. It catches the sun for a second, but it's not as good as the knife, which sends sparkles round the breakfast table.

He gets up quickly, wiping his mouth, and says simply, "I gotta go." The clock confirms this; college time. The West Greenstead and Ditchling College time. I see him in the yard, opening the shed where his bicycle is kept, and as his trousers press tightly against him as he mounts the saddle, I think how beautiful he is. I would like to be that saddle now - I am deeply envious of it, holding him, supporting him, as I sway beneath him. His mop of dark hair and long arms crouch over the handlebars, and the bicycle is out of sight, on its way to the college catering department, leaving me alone in the house now.

I put the breakfast dishes in the washing-up bowl; his dishes, mine, merged together in an aquatic sprawl – my dishes lying on top of his.

He will be cycling over the level crossing, feeling the divots as the bike thuds down hard on them, and, with a glance to the left – I'm sure it will be the left – he looks up the empty railway line. It had better be empty, there have been too many accidents of late….. and talking of accidents…

Once the dishes are drying neatly on the rack I climb upstairs, softly, as I always do, in case anyone is about. The door to Rory's room is closed, so I turn the handle gently and slip inside. Immediately I'm inside the room there is a smell of Rory – a good smell, a distinctive smell. The room is in half-light, as if awaiting the presence of a lover; curtains half-drawn, the bed unmade. The window is open, leaving some of Rory to seep into the garden.

There is a pair of football shorts and a red T-shirt on a chair, but he hasn't worn these for a few weeks now as the season ended. Instead, there are the gruff spikes of cricket boots, but alas the whites in which he looks so cute – dark on white – are nowhere to be seen. Neatly stowed away in a cupboard, in readiness for the first game.

I can see him running in, dark hair flopping, and with this pleasing image, I take off my shoes and socks, all my clothes, thrown quickly into a little bundle, and dive into his bed.

There is Rory on the sheets and on the pillow. The unmade bed is cool and welcoming. It's like jumping into foreign waters, both different and familiar, as I splay around in delight in my new domain.

Suddenly the garden gate goes click, and for a moment I freeze in panic; the rasping sound of the letterbox and the clattering of falling mail announces the postman at the door. I slink back under the covers and then, to add to my panic, the bell rings. What am I going to do? What does he want? There's a long silence and I tiptoe softly to the window, cool in my new nakedness, to peep through the curtain chink.

The postman's in a strange position, stooping or something – but then who am I to talk? Look where I am, an interloper in another's bedroom. I get dressed, rumbled in part by the unsuspecting postman, (or is he?), who leaves the gate open and disappears down the lane.

I click the door gently to, goodbye for now to the realm of Rory, who must be at college, bending to lock his bike in the ramshackle bicycle shed.

I once suggested that we got a tandem, but he rejected it out of hand, called me a wimp and said it would be him doing all the cycling. Much better perhaps to ride two on one, I thought afterwards in consolation.

So this is my morning routine to slide into...

I'm packing my bag. It's not too late, and if I run, I can catch the bus that goes from round the corner. It's time for me to go to college, only no cakes and pastry or waiting on simulated customers, just books and poems and a slimline volume of Voltaire's letters. French at 3.

I wonder what time it was in the room, the room I told you about, when she came in – for it must have been a she. The moment that changed all our destinies, singly and as constellations, and sent me ricocheting off in another quite different direction.

'How can you know?' I hear you say, for you wouldn't be the first. This is some kind of fantasy, just like... But on both counts I'd beg to differ. And as for the second, it's a reality too, for I stole into a bed, a real bed, before the postman came to interrupt everything.

The reason I came to know is because I eavesdropped. Two aunts talking... A private conversation in the summer house and, well I'd returned home early from college unannounced. Mr. Touquet was ill, so Voltaire had the afternoon off, being left to languish in my locker and according me a double period of freedom. I'd planned to surprise them and sneak right up on them, but something made me stop and I hovered for a moment behind the hedge.

"Gemma thinks so more and more," I could hear Jane say. Her listener gave a mild affirmative grunt. "She thinks there was a mix up, a muddle, and somehow they got swapped round."

"But what about the labels, surely? They always have."

"Well..." A silence. The grass was tickling my shoes.

"It may have been done deliberately," a voice said after a while. "After all, she could never be sure."

"But who...?"

The sentence vanished in mid-air as I ran back in shock towards the house. I'd heard enough.

And then I knew. Well perhaps I'd always known. Looking at photographs seemed to convince me all the more.

So that was when I started to look at him closely, to go into his room. For if he wasn't my brother, then it wasn't the same and it wasn't wrong to look at him; to watch him after a shower, drying himself off. He always left his bedroom door ajar, as if he were proud or wanted to be discovered – proud of his prowess, which in turn hypnotised and fascinated me. Only when he leaves for college, when he leaves the house, does he shut his room – as you already know.

And then a little voice says, "But he is your brother, you've grown up with him."

And another voice says, "But it's not the same, the same blood, so you can." Same blood!

I like that voice, and as I listen to it, I close my eyes, feeling those invisible hands lifting me up, taking off the labels, lifting me... changing me forever.

The Right Sort

"George!" said Norma, sharply, "Come away from that window."

"Just a minute," replied George, curtain twitching, "I think they've arrived."

They both looked intently from either side of the window, half concealed by the curtains.

A well-dressed woman was walking up the path of the house next door. The neat semi-detached had been empty for some while. They could see her fumbling with a key.

"You're right," said Norma. "I don't see anyone else though."

"No."

"She looks quite decent," Norma remarked. "Better than that man who worked for London Transport."

"He was alright," remonstrated George.

"Oh no, he wasn't. The language! And that bag he used to carry round with him. Made him look like the plumber."

George had no weapons to counter such irrefutable arguments, but he noticed that for the rest of the evening, Norma hummed around the house in an unusually good mood.

It was the next day when Norma met her new neighbour coming up the path. She was not alone. Her elegantly tinted hair met with her warm approval. As one elegant lady to another, Norma knew good taste when she saw it. She threw a radiant smile at the newcomer who reciprocated and pointed behind her.

"Hello," she said. "These are my four daughters. Christine, Marie, Sophie and Etienne."

Norma looked shyly at four very tall and attractive girls. They smiled together as a unit.

"And I am Constance Lamot," the new neighbour continued.

"Norma Wilkinson," said Norma. "Pleased to meet you." Then, recovering her inquisitiveness, "And Mr. Lamot?"

"Oh my dear," said Constance wistfully. "You'll hardly ever see him. He's so often away on business."

Norma nodded sympathetically.

The following morning, when they were eating their raspberries in front of the telly, they saw Mr. Lamot leave the house.

He was, as Norma imagined, a smart, well-dressed man with a trim beard and immaculate suit. He carried a long umbrella.

She hurried out into the front garden on the pretext of rescuing a punnet from underneath one of the bushes. As she went out she called over to him in her friendliest voice. At first he didn't appear to hear her, so Norma pursued him along the fence.

He turned around slightly apprehensively.

"Just moved in have you?" Norma cooed.

The man looked perplexed. From his position at the window, George saw him smile frequently and shake his head. But soon Norma came back into the house dejectedly.

"He doesn't speak any English!" she wailed.

"Dear me, how could he!" replied George. "By the way, is there any more cream?"

The following weeks passed fairly pleasantly and uneventfully with the new neighbours, though it seemed to Norma that next door's bell was always ringing.

"She's a bit strict," Norma remarked. "She doesn't even give her daughters a key."

The next day saw a lorry pull up outside the house. A batch of small garden canes was being delivered.

"George." She nudged him from his newspaper. "It looks like they plan on making a go of the garden. That means you'll have to get out in ours more often."

"Yes," said George.

A day or so later, when she was out in the garden making plans for the cabbage patch, she heard a dreadful screeching coming from next door.

She stood bolt upright, secateurs in hand. A window was opened. Then there was the sound of heated voices and of something being knocked over. To her surprise, she saw a pair of trousers come flying out the window. They landed on top of the rhubarb in her garden.

"Uggh!" groaned Norma.

Then came a shirt and two socks, followed by a blonde wig. The wailing grew louder. Terrified, she ran back inside the house, clutching her secateurs, and firmly bolted the back door. Quivering nervously, she peered from her kitchen window, but everything was quiet now. Birds were beginning to re-appear on the lawn.

When George came back that evening she told him about everything that had gone on. But in his usual dismissive way he said calmly, "They're foreign dear, and a bit more excitable than we are. That's all."

Norma remained unconvinced. "What shall we do about the trousers? We can't have them in our garden."

"Take them back," he suggested. "They look quite an expensive pair."

Norma thought for a moment. "No George. I think it would be better if you took them back. Supposing somebody spotted me. What would they think?"

"Put them in a bag," he volunteered.

However Norma had decided.

"Where are they?" he mumbled grudgingly.

"In the garden by the rhubarb. On the other hand, maybe you should wait until it gets dark."

So George waited until the onset of darkness, and at a little after half past nine, he stole across the lawn, hoping that at that moment no one was looking out of their bedroom window.

To his surprise, however, the disreputable pair of trousers had disappeared. Instead, all he could see lying on the ground was a small white card. It bore the name Henrik van Eyck, architect.

George and Norma were mystified by the whole thing. The sudden disappearance of the trousers was as uncanny as the revelation of the white card.

Nearly a week later, Norma learned that the Lamots had suddenly moved, although a number of distinguished looking gentlemen kept calling at the house.

It was her task, if the ringing persisted for too long, to send them away with the sad news that the Lamots had indeed moved.

On one occasion, she even used an old Japanese phrase book she had bought in a jumble sale.

"I knew they were no good," she said one evening when George was listening to Stars on Sunday.

"How's that?" said George, "I thought you said they were decent people."

"Maybe," said Norma. "Maybe," putting away the Japanese book. "But they never did do the garden, did they? And after ordering all those bamboo canes."

"It's typical," she continued, as George turned up the radio to a volume that ensured privacy. "It's all show."

From the Door

She awakes now. The room is there. In slow motion it adjusts itself and is revealed as the sombre, heavily furnished room, letting in winter light. She gets out of bed, groggy, half drunk, the cold floor serving as a reminder that it is all over now.

From the other side of the bed, the side where Mark has lain, she sees the crumpled pattern of sheets. Anna draws back the curtain fully, and now her feet are fast becoming colder. She welcomes it, though not the ensuing numbness. Snow falls on the other side of the window. The dream recedes, has gone. Daybreak.

It's a long way to the nearest store, but Anna will have to go there later, only she hopes the snow will not set in, adding more time to the winding, tortuous roads.

The kettle sings on the stove, which sends its warmth across the kitchen. It's a good companion in winter – its ever readiness to heat a soup, accommodate a kettle. Through the window, the flakes are subsiding, only a thin covering on this late October day. But there will be more to come, this being the harbinger of winter.

"Hi, honey!" Mark comes in from his wood-logging, his face ruddy from the cold, his nose like something a clown would wear. "Is there tea on?"

She nods. She doesn't tell him about the dream as he would only worry, but she hopes he doesn't notice that she is still recovering, for the dream takes its toll. Like a bad drug whose effects take hours to wear off.

"You going to the store?"

She nods. "What do you need?"

In half an hour, he is away again – the surrounding woods provide an endless source of work, and now the days are shorter, he must get up early to profit from the daylight hours.

The key is in the ignition, the car chokes and starts. In her mind's eye, she can see them, surrounded by them.

She judders like the engine and in a moment is sailing slowly down the hill, as if sailing can ever describe a journey by car. Almost soundlessly, the car slides down the everlasting hill. For two and a half miles she will not have to use a drop of petrol as the road curves and turns. She smiles. Her grandfather would approve, seeing as he was thrift personified.

In the store they haven't much, but she makes the most of what they do have. She'll cook something from her Hungarian cookbook, with lashings of paprika.

"Someone likes their food spicy," the woman in the shop says.

"Winter's coming," Anna says. "Why not?"

She puts her provisions in the boot and heads back for home. So far, no more snow, but as the weather can turn very suddenly in this hilly region, she wastes no time.

The woman waves. "See you next week."

Back in the cabin she prepares the ingredients. In no time at all, it's gone again. Mark is ravenous from the chilly air and eats three bowls of paprikaš. He falls asleep in the chair in front of the Aga while Anna reads her book.

"You'd better turn in," she says.

"You coming?" he murmurs.

"I won't be long. Just five more pages."

Again he's asleep when she enters the room. As she falls into bed, she pleads silently for a moment. "Please don't let it come again. Please let it be a calm night."

The temperature falls and they sleep like ones who have hibernated. Anna awakes refreshed from a dreamless sleep. Mark is already up. In the night there was a heavy fall of snow.

The air is silent now, no wind, and the woods are covered in a wrap of wool. Anna works inside the house and, after the midday soup, she leaves the cabin to take a walk.

The air is still with the threat of more snow and even though her breath unfurls in little balls of cloud, it does not feel that cold. She takes a detour from her usual path, where the trees are more tightly packed together, some deciduous mixed in with pine. She goes right down to the bottom, across the frozen stream, now covered in a deep, white blanket.

She begins the ascent, the steep slope, the snow in heavy drifts.

Suddenly she gives a start. To her right, in a thicker clump of trees, she can see the eyes of some wild animal looking at her. Anna stops, frozen to the ground. She is in the dream now, but there is only one of them. She must try and run through the thick snow.

All at once there is a tearing sound, a cracking – a deep, heavy thud. Blood rushes to her head and the wood goes very dark.

She awakes now in another white place. There is something attached to her arm. She is unable to move. A white figure, a sort of angel floats towards her.

"Would you like to see your husband now?"

Anna nods, still not comprehending where she is. Mark comes in with a small bunch of flowers – where did he get them this time of year? He sits beside her.

"You gave me quite a fright," he says.

"What happened?" she asks.

"A branch came down on you in the snow. It was with the weight. You were in quite a state."

Silence. Bright flowers.

"How long am I going to have to be here?"

"A few more days. You took a nasty blow. Do you remember anything?"

"Yes, I remember it all, except getting here."

When he leaves, he gives her a kiss.

"See you tomorrow."

It's not nice, she thinks, to be alone in bed. She misses his warm body, the way he curves into her at night.

"Only a few more days," she tells herself.

Next day there is a party at her bedside. The expressions are serious, no joviality, no false banter.

"Mrs. Kerr," says the surgeon, "I'm afraid you'll have to be here a little longer."

She feels anxious, her prison term extended.

"When we did our examination," he says softly, "we found a growth."

The room goes white and cold. She is lying out in the snow.

"It'll mean more tests."

The afternoon is an age. A grey cold view from her window. She waits for Mark, and wants to cry, but she can only do this when he's there. She misses the cabin and the warm stove in the hills and the tap-tapping of trees being felled in the woods. The ride to the store on her 'grandfather's petrol', and she wants to be rid of the painful drip in her arm.

Mark comes. She cries. He holds her. The visitors disperse. He stays late, draws the curtains round the bed and holds her to the latest hour. At last she falls asleep, whereupon he leaves, to return tomorrow.

From her window she can see the next day is warmer. There's a fine, grey drizzle in the air, which gives way to rain. It'll melt the snow, she thinks, and already the view from the large ward window is admitting streaks of grey and brown, leading towards the slushy avenues.

When she stayed at her grandparents', she used to love the rain at night. She slept in a small bedroom under the roof and the rain dripped down the gutters and splashed onto the pipes. They lived near a wood too, a smallholding at the end of a lane which led nowhere. It was nice because no traffic flew past, only bikers, and walkers in thick socks and clumpy waterproof boots. Her grandfather was always in the garden, always growing things.

One morning, after a spring shower, whose soothing rain had sent her back to sleep, she found him planting lettuces in the large border.

"Elsie disapproves, but I likes to use the space."

The dibber made another hole. He stood up to face her, to smile at his favourite granddaughter.

"All helps to keep the wolf from the door," he grinned.

She looked back at the swaying flowers, uncomprehending. The wolf?

Anna could see herself standing in that garden, long, long before she ever came to Canada.

She lay very still for a moment, the snow outside the window receding. Her grandfather's words, words – those dreams… And finally she understood it all.

The predatory shapes that haunted her, relentlessly, persistently, were now unmasked.

The ward seemed much clearer, vivid even. The male nurse, who came to ask her if she wanted anything, had beautiful eyes.

She felt her left breast gingerly, wondering how much longer it would still be there. In two hours' time, Mark would be on his way.

The wind tapped the window. The blood within her was bubbling, ready to fight falling trees, snow, the growth that had crept up on her slowly, stealthily… Even the wolf.

Vegetable Plot

It seemed to her that the back gardens were fast becoming like a market place. Eileen Corton peered out of the living room at the assorted heads on either side of the fence. Wiping her breath away from the window, she gazed more intently upon the scene. Savoy cabbages were being held up for inspection, each one eliciting a soft murmur of approval. Little round marbles identified as cherry tomatoes; stubby shaped potatoes. What was happening out there? Were they going to set up a stall? Her garden, however, had little to offer on the vegetable side. There was some scraggy rhubarb, but that was about it. Otherwise, the drooping hollyhocks that bordered either side of the garden were her main exhibit.

"Come on," she called to the cat nestling at her ankles, luring it as it lazily plodded into the kitchen. It buried its head in a familiar bowl and there was an odd munching sound as she spied through the window again. Eileen was beginning to get nettled by the vegetable community. Sometimes they stood there gabbling for hours; each day produced a new lecture. She fell asleep during Stars on Sunday and afterwards wearily climbed the stairs to bed.

The next day dawned bright and sunny, and, in positive mood, Eileen decided to make overtures to the leguminous community. She would start a conversation with Mrs. Logan, whose ample backside hovered beneath apple tree and washing line. It seemed to be grazing like a giant bumble bee as it swayed from side to side. She stepped out into the garden to address its serene posture. "Lovely day," she began, as the sun slipped behind a cloud.

The buttocks quivered but there was no answer.

"Lovely, isn't it?" she repeated.

There was still no reply. Having forgotten that Mavis Logan was rather deaf, she took the stubborn silence of the ignorant posterior to be some kind of snub. Going back inside, she gazed for a while out of the window. Washing now formed a barrier to the sun, blotting out sky and poplars alike. The battery of Logan long johns, vests and assorted knickers oppressed her. In the aftermath, she felt hurt and excluded.

A few days later, there was another assembly at the bottom of next-door's garden. Various fingers pointed to an object below the greenhouse, and there were exclamations of, "Oh, how lovely!" and, "Coming on nicely now." They all bent down simultaneously to examine the prize object. Mr. Logan, like a proud father, fished out his watering can and began to spray it. Gradually, they drifted back into the house, with the exception of Henry Logan, who stood wondrously admiring the invisible masterpiece.

Eileen thought she too would venture out into the garden, pick a few dahlias and satisfy her curiosity. Stepping out onto the lawn, she executed a couple of cursory snips and drew nearer to the greenhouse. She approached the fence, and, as if by chance, glanced over.

At first, she couldn't see anything, so she stared at the greenfly on one of the rosebuds and then turned round again. Lying heavily under a collection of dark green leaves, and with one yellow flower, was an enormous marrow. It looked like some kind of oxygen cylinder, green and sparkling with the water that had been sprinkled on it.

"Oh, splendid!" she beamed across to Henry Logan, who seemed lost in admiration. He glanced up. "Oh, hello... yes..."

"I wondered what you were all looking at..." she began.

There was the sound of a phone ringing from somewhere, whereupon Mr. Logan suddenly became attentive. "That'll be mine. Probably Sid from the allotment. Back in a minute."

He hurried towards the house, casting a fleeting glimpse back towards the marrow, and disappeared through the French windows. Eileen stood alone in the garden with only the dahlias and the marrow for company. A blackbird sang softly behind the fence, but she didn't hear it. Snipping a couple more plants, she waited a while and then went back inside.

"What was the point?" she muttered gloomily and settled down to watch TV.

During the evening, the marrow returned to haunt her. She saw Mr. and Mrs. Logan running back into the house. She hated that marrow. Even though she sat back in her chair and tried to ignore it, it kept reappearing at odd intervals. During a programme on U-boats, she became convinced that what she was looking at was none other than a giant version of an underwater courgette. Hurriedly, she changed channels. "Zucchini," said a bucolic voice. It was too much. She switched off, her evening ruined. Unless...

It was some while later when she crept out again into the garden. The fence between hers and the next-door garden was low. She could easily climb it. As she landed in the adjoining garden, the pair of shears she was carrying momentarily brushed the soil. The moon lit up the glass panels of the greenhouse. It would be easy to locate that offensive vegetable. Something scuttled away beneath the shrubs as she stood in front of the impressive spread of marrow, then she bent down, gripping the shears tightly in her hand.

One decisive snip and that was it. The marrow slid away from its stem, lying heavy and Zeppelin-like on top of its crushed leaves. Glaring at it for a moment, Eileen picked it up and hurled it furiously over the fence. It flew briefly through the air then plummeted. There was a deep splashing sound. It had landed either in the pond at the bottom of the garden or in the Thompson's cold frame. The wildlife chattered away to itself indignantly, then all was quiet.

It was about midday when the theft was discovered. The police were called but they never thought to drain the pond. The marrow had vanished without trace.

For days, a funereal silence hung over the adjacent gardens, punctuated only by the odd Logan expletive. Yet Eileen noticed that if anything, the kidnapping of the marrow only served to strengthen the vegetable community. There was an abiding feeling of vigilant solidarity, and even after she'd been to confession for the third time, Eileen still admitted to a pervading sense of guilt.

She felt as if they held her permanently under suspicion, as a result of which, she seldom let the cat, which clung more assiduously than ever to her ankles, stray out alone at night.

Us

Now where was I? Oh, yes. Yes, you could look on it like this. A kind of... well, privatisation perhaps. Popular word that, nowadays. All sorts of unlikely commodities ending up in single pockets. Did I say pockets? I meant hands. Even the gentle drops of dew from heaven – it's back in fashion, by the way – diverted into special companies, only to leak back through antiquated pipes into the lush soil.

I'm well read, you can see. But I digress. So the order came from... well, over there. Just follow my finger. It was costing far too much – too much to run. I know the leadership seemed new and dynamic to you, especially when they'd buried three old men on the trot. You felt you could do business with them – not my words, of course. But actually, the idea came long before that.

Your other question. What were those fences keeping out? I prefer state boundary myself, but have it your way. Mostly the alarms were being set off by stray partridges and woodpigeons, the occasional deer, or the odd East German. It was costing far too much. Can you imagine how much? Way over budget. Them, us, everybody.

So what we did, we thought we'd have a change of personnel. A revolution orchestrated to a simple theme. A spontaneous outpouring. And then, waiting in the wings when the ancient men had gone... you guessed it! Us! Made to look so logical and natural, but to tell you the truth we'd been waiting in those wings for far too long, so that we were getting old too.

Yes, so just when I was looking forward to having my name on the door, the whole thing went round again. Ha! It makes me laugh, but do you know what it used to say on the revolving door of the university library? Revolution for Academics. Quite droll that. And appropriate. Cosmetic, ineffectual. And that's what we planned to do. Just the same; merely change the names.

But then the bastards did it again. Wouldn't budge until our special selection was unfrocked. This, frankly, was quite unnerving; a second click of the cog. Now that's not supposed to happen. Is it? Is it? I should remind you, it's us who do the hijacking.

Thank you, Maria. Yes, could you put it over there? I won't be too long. Just tying up a few loose ends. And yes, I won't forget to drink it.

Her concern for me is quite touching. I think she too was most upset by the second click of the wheel. Yes. Hails from the mountains, where we had our second summer home.

Anyway, there we were; all new faces. Slightly younger, perhaps; less serious; smiling even. But still they went on strike again. On strike! Said they didn't want any of our sort. Said they'd had too much of us for far too long. Well, we disagreed. Said you can't have too much of a good thing. And we knew best. From where we could see, yes, we knew best.

Momentarily, we were looking to use all our powers of persuasion – in the old days it would have been unthinkable – but now... It never came to that... unlike in some places I could care to mention. After all, we have a tradition of reasonableness here.

So the strike booted us out. Put the mockers on the carefully laid plans.

The square was full to capacity. A sea of arms and voices. Something we'd taught them to do, but of course we tempered it with our icons. Every year the heroes of the parade grew younger. Miraculously, the ageing process was halted. Bald heads became a little more shaggy; sagging jowls a shade more angular; bold eyes containing a braver, brighter vision.

Of course, you're right. I freely admit it. The idea came from the incense swingers. Everything was replicated. Same thing, same time of year even. Same, but sweetly different.

Look now. The priests have no congregation. They've gone

elsewhere; forced to live like monks in solitude. But then, what a waste! Why should we forgo life's little pleasures? After all, there's all my knowledge. A wealth of experience tempered by an experience of wealth. All stashed away, too. Don't forget, we were the ones who could travel. We made the rules, the boundaries... What else is there to do in Switzerland? I ask you! A land so clean that no one lives there. Cuckoo clocks and chocolate boxes. I made my trips to the Institute discreetly, quietly.

That cake was delicious, by the way. Pity you didn't get some.

Second click of the cog.

I then had to make my way alone... And very nicely I'm doing, too. I've got my own little concern; my money-spinner; financed by some appropriate and appropriated funds. I gather you've had the same thing too. All your various commodities: gas, water, telephone; the lot. So here I am. I'm back in business. Look upon it as if I never went away.

We're all here in fact, in one form or another. They dare not touch us. We know too much...

Fully privatised yet individual now. We all are.

And that's the way it is. Yes, we'll show you – the way, that is – we'll show you. You can rely on us. It'll be our pleasure.

Buoyant

I am heavier in the morning, I know. As I move from the bumpy springs of my bed, I sense I am scattered on the surf of another day. The curtains drawn back reveal a pale yard lit in sun. The yard is full of dust, blown up from the farm.

Emmanuel is already in the field.

I have never told him. Easy, you would think, but not easy to confide in the one who knows you.

I slink like a slug onto the cold, stone floor. The cold runs up through my ankles, supporting the rest of me, and the cold pain gives way to comfort. Pain means I'm not alone, and, as the farmhouse clock ticks eight o'clock, I am slowly descending the wooden staircase, listening to each incisive creak. Every creak is me, but when *he* stands on each polished stair, the noise is oh, so different.

Breakfast takes place with a little party of friends assembled there to greet me. The china jug with the crack just below the spout. The neat row of cup, saucer, plate; the bread nestling coyly in its basket.

He's long had his, out in the fields to meet the varying light of day – he'll be back late, or maybe at lunch to meet me, except on this day I won't be there. He'll scratch his head and then say, "Oh yes, the market." He'll see me behind a barrowload of cheeses, the stale sex smell of the seafood stall, and the china junk table with everything priced…

But no, he won't see me.

At eleven o'clock I'll collect my coat, buttoning it gently round me, breathing in for a second as I close the door behind me, listening to its soft, impersonal click, a click that says neither goodbye nor welcome – a click that is merely a click.

The bus will take me into town; from the lonely bus shelter in the square, I am the only passenger till we pass the library. But the library is shut today, I remember, and so my lone vigil goes on. A bus to myself, a multitude of seats with no one for me to squash against, or feel their unspoken sighs, as I tilt in my ungainly way on my path to the soft leather.

The seat squishes as it heeds my contact, but for me there is more squish than most. Empty, all to myself, the bus, the driver cocooned in his thug-proof cubicle, the solitary boatman to whom I've paid the fare.

There, I've thought about it again, just when I wasn't going to.

Emmanuel is in the field, looking up at the dwindling hedgerows. The neighbours pulled them out. They have no sense and no need of them, it seems. Ours were covered in stray birds – for a while – and then they were gone. The prairiefication had already started – fewer trees gave less space in which to hide myself. Those people came and didn't know the land. It was just a fat cow to be sucked dry. Dry!

And I'm sure they made the climate change. Slowly, very gradually. Emmanuel said I imagined it, but prairies are such cold places. Not like welcome spinneys on a warm, wet afternoon.

But I'm on the bus now, as I said, passing giant razors and golden butter.

I remembered a poem – a knife, golden gutter or butter, or perhaps it was the other way round.

My solitary chauffeur turns round to greet me. It is the end. "Terminus," he says. Silly of me to have forgotten. 'And high above the golden gutter, a something knife sinks into something butter'. No, it wasn't that word, I'm sure.

He has delivered me, and already his arms are straining at the wheel. I cast a look at his eyes and think, he's not bad, but he won't have thought the same of me. What is there to wonder about a wobbly pear?

Slowly, I step along the egg box cobbles, done purposefully to trip you up. I negotiate each one carefully. I'm walking therefore on tiny mushrooms, upturned stone circles. I look up, but I can see no sun in this maze of interlocking streets. I'm still climbing, climbing, past the chapel at the bend in the road, and for a second I stare back, seeing all before me.

Emmanuel, if he's not gone home, will be sitting on a tree trunk having his lunch. Idyllic really. I can see him among the reeds and whispering grasses.

I turn my eyes from the pictured sandwich, the sharp, white teeth with never a filling, and the golden apple plucked from one of our own espalier trees.

I can hear the murmur of an engine, and at the next bend my eyes are looking at water. Real water. I close them for a second, then look again.

The boats below look tiny, like little stranded moths skimming the water. And in their wake, their ruffled paths cause the driftwood to bob against the shore.

I'm out of breath as perhaps I told you. Or maybe I didn't. I could have held that back. Perhaps you won't want to see me, hot and bothered, little drops of sweat gathering round my eyes. And I am out of breath for I was climbing, climbing.

I'm sailing now, in a manner of speaking, past the chimneys of the town, the red characteristic pantiles, and, in the wake of the great lumbering turtle, who leaves no ripples, I can sense the eyes drifting on me, watching me, as they always have, with amusement... and derision.

I hold onto one side and step up on to a small stone plinth. From here my path will be easy. The breeze will cool my sweat, those little beads of dew and indignity that have gathered round. Gather round.

As I step out, the wind is blowing quite a gale, so that I reach out to clasp a girder to steady me on my way.

Ironic really that I should be so careful. After all...

Now the moths are below my ankles. I can see them, bobbing, swirling. Bobbing – I like that word.

The breeze blows, and I shall join them in a last descent. And as I slide through the air, I shall be feather-light, and this great cumbersome body will float upon the water, lighter than air.

Will bob and float upon the water... lighter, brighter than air.

The Silence

"They said he was even better than his old man," Bill had said to her one afternoon when she'd come back in from the garden. May looked blankly at him as he jerked a thumb in the direction of the radio. She had no idea what the music was, nor the name he had suddenly spouted.

As soon as the news came on, he turned the radio off, it being his cue to come out and see what she'd done in the greenhouse.

"Bloody wars," he had said, "nothing but bloody wars!" Then looking at the rows of potted cuttings, "You done well, girl," and he'd invariably ruffle her hair like a schoolgirl and smile.

May shuddered. It was lonely now in the greenhouse, despite the late autumn sun. Lonely too in the house for that matter, ever since… She put down the secateurs and gave them a brief wipe. The soil that had accumulated on them fell as powder, and she spooned it up carefully with her hands to put it back into the sack.

"Compost never came cheap," Bill had said once, nodding sagely at the time.

Stepping into the kitchen, she could hear his voice saying, "potting". Potting without the 't's'. Po'ing, po'ing, po'ing. May stood there for a moment. Going, going, gone, she sighed, locking the back door as he'd always told her to.

The room was silent, still – frozen in time. It was the noise she missed most, for Bill was always listening to music, humming tunes. "You're eiver a hummer, or you're not," he'd said. "Some people sing and some don't."

"Yes, dear," she said, making the tea. Another wisp of wisdom, for she could scarcely remember the last time she had sung.

Guiltily now, she switched on the TV, and sat down with her tea and biscuits. It was a game show, her favourite – something Bill would never have liked or watched even. It had been Joan who had persuaded her to get the 'box'. "Bit of company," she said, "and now lots of programmes are in colour. You'd love it for the gardening." The last words had clinched it. The thrill of seeing all those fuchsias and bright red begonias. Never seen anything like it! And sometimes they went out to visit stately homes and gardens. Tours of herbaceous borders accompanied by solemn music. The kind Bill liked. And as for Last Night of the Proms...

The game show was breaking for adverts, so she got up and nipped to the loo. After all, that's what adverts are for, she'd told Joan in her first week of telly ownership. That's what them things are for.

It was damp the next morning when she awoke. Clouds of drizzle blew across the garden, so gazing out of the window, she decided she would have to change her plans. Of course it was tempting just to sit in front of the telly, but she'd made a rule, a sort of 'deal with 'im', who, if he could see her now... No viewing before 4 o'clock. Get out the house, girl, she'd said to herself. And she did.

The street was rainy, rained-on. Forty minutes would take her in to town, ten by bus, but she was in no hurry, and the air, for all its dampness, would do her good.

She walked down the tree-lined street, looking at the new, green litterbins with smiley faces. This was the bit of town with houses set back from the road, cars instead of plants in the front gardens. Then, at the roundabout, it all changed, as if the leafy avenue had been a mistake, an afterthought, and it all reverted to the original plan. The street began to narrow, flanked by boarded-up buildings. Then the odd pub on the corner with its creaking sign, a chippie, blousy take-away. Otherwise, the shops she knew had gone.

The bus overtook her at the swimming pool, displaying a row of solemn heads in profile. She was pleased to have got so far, and to have saved the money. It could go towards a packet of seeds, as she meant to stop by Eric the ironmonger's after she'd been to the library.

As she climbed the steps to both town hall and library, she noticed that the fountain was not playing that morning. She liked to listen to its splash of jets and sit on one of the benches arranged round it, but now the morning brought only damp drizzle and there was hardly anyone around. Pushing at the revolving door, she was now in the vestibule of the library; an enormous bare entrance. The book she'd finished was given over to the assistant as she headed off in search of another. "You can take up to eight," they'd said to her once, but she shook her head. The one would do, besides she wouldn't know which one to start with.

At the 'out' counter she put her ticket down on top of the book and waited.

"It isn't the right one," the assistant said. "It's for the music library."

"Music library?" She looked again, and holding the card up she saw Bill's signature not hers.

"Where is the music library?" she asked and followed the direction of an outstretched finger. "Keep that book for me, will you?" as she made her way gingerly up the staircase to the music section.

Glancing through the large panes of glass, it looked quite nice, smaller than the main library and it had long, blue curtains tapering down the windows. Tentatively, she pushed open the door. There was no one to disturb here, just an odour of wood and polished floors, a waft of cardboard sleeves containing vinyl. Then she detected another smell, as she looked around, a strangely familiar smell. It took her a few minutes to work out what it was as she walked over to the unattended counter. Bill's raincoat. That's what it was. A musty smell of raincoat.

As she looked again at his name on the ticket, she realised that he'd never once told her that he belonged to the music library. She'd often wondered why it took him so long to come back home from town, and now the answer lay in her hand, in the form of his frayed and worn out library card.

Why had he never bothered to tell her? she wondered, as her eyes alighted on three sets of tables with adjacent headphones. Perhaps he thought she'd make fun of him for listening to more stuff when he already listened to the radio at home.

"Does the headphones mean I can listen to it here?" she asked a tall, slim boy emerging from behind the counter. He nodded.

"And where do I choose the records?"

He pointed towards the window. "There's a catalogue over there. We've got cassettes now too."

May looked over again at the three seats and wondered which one was his – which would have been his favourite one. She judged it to be the one on the left.

"In his time they reckoned him better than his old man." She recalled his words and wondered who he was talking about. She'd like to listen to something that he'd listened to, but she couldn't remember any of the names.

"My 'usband used to come here," she said, straying back to the counter. "Did you know 'im?"

The boy smiled and shook his head. "Sorry, but I've not been here that long. Just a couple of weeks. What was the name?"

"Burton. William Burton."

"Maybe some of the other staff would know."

"I want to listen to something he might have listened to," May announced.

"Of course." He waited for her to volunteer more information.

"Someone who wrote music and whose dad did too."

The young man tried to restrain a smile and thought for a moment. "Well now, Scarlatti, Strauss, Mozart even and Bach."

"The last one," she said, as if suddenly jolted. "The Bach."

"The father or the son?"

"He said he liked the son." She followed him over to the catalogue, neat rows of cards in wooden drawers.

"Well, take your pick," he said. "J.C, W.F, Emmanuel."

"Emmanuel," she replied. "I'd like to listen to the Emmanuel."

As she took a seat, she was none the wiser as to how to work the things. She sat hesitantly as the boy adjusted the headphones for her. He had nice eyes, she thought, as he bent down in front of her, and a nice, slim body just like... she smiled. There was a strange hissing sound in her ears, followed by a bang that made her jump.

"Too loud?" he asked, and twiddled a switch on the left. "Better now?" he mouthed, and May nodded.

Gazing at the lime tree beyond the window, she sat back to listen to the music. It went very fast but it had a good rhythm. Her foot began tapping away involuntarily, even if it kept stopping and starting all the time. And some snatches of it even sounded familiar – perhaps Bill had hummed it to her when they were sitting there in the kitchen. Now it went abruptly from fast to slow, and she sat back and closed her eyes.

She was coming in from the garden, the kettle was on, and he was waving time to the music. She spread her hand out as he came towards her, then held it, gently at first, very gently, then clasped it brightly, tight...

Wilf

Every week, she would go to the large department store in the centre of town. Every Wednesday, she stepped across plush carpets under the screeching drone of the air-conditioning to perform the same ritual.

In the yellow cubicle she would try on a dress and then hand it back to the assistant. This was accompanied by a wistful expression and a shaking of the head. Sometimes she would leave the store having purchased a towel or a box of tissues, but nothing more.

One day, when she was in the cubicle, she had a strange sensation, like a hand rubbing lightly against her shoulder. Glynis pulled at the hem of her dress and saw, quite clearly in the mirror, a hand. It was ownerless. She looked again and saw it was fondling the nape of her neck. Glynis breathed a little sigh. It seemed to have friendly intentions. Handing back the dress to the assistant, she decided to keep quiet about the hand. After all, who would have believed her?

Returning the following day, more out of curiosity, she experienced the same thing. Slipping off her shoes, she noticed a wayward palm massaging her leg with its long fingernails. It then slid up her leg and reappeared suddenly by her ear, being content to tickle her lobe.

Whether it was a male or female hand, she couldn't really tell. Moreover, she neither cared, for it was a change nowadays to find a hand with a pleasant and friendly disposition. After all, it was really rather attentive. When it had massaged her neck and chased away any oncoming headaches, she handed back the dress to the assistant.

She made several pilgrimages to the store and experienced many pleasant moments with the hand, whom she now referred to as Wilf. At times, she thought there was more than one hand there, but this was entirely due to Wilf's successful technique. The long fingernails brightened up many a dull, wet afternoon.

One day, however, she was called away unexpectedly to a soufflé conference in Bodmin. It was nearly six weeks before she returned.

When she walked back across the carpets of her favourite store, she found, to her horror, that everything had changed. The hanky department had disappeared, and her own counter had been moved further round. At least, to her relief, the cubicle remained.

But when she moved a fraction closer, she found the door had been painted a different colour and a collecting box had been placed outside.

"What's this for?" she asked a bright-eyed woman sitting at a table.

"Changing fee. To cover overheads."

She felt in her pockets and pulled out a twenty-pence piece.

"Not enough."

"Not enough? What do you mean, not enough?"

"The fee is ten percent of all purchases made."

"But how do you know I'm going to buy anything?" she replied.

"I'm afraid that's not my problem, dear."

And Glynis sadly thought of the hand behind the door and went in search of other department stores, wondering at the same time if Wilf had been a willing accomplice to such artless exploitation.

Bonhomie

It's the bonhomie that gets me, thought Joe morosely, glancing at cheese straws perched precariously in tumblers. Spread-eagled in different parts of the room, mosaics of canapés were positioned next to the harsher, more jagged outlines of tortilla chips.

Joe sighed. The inevitable Christmas party. A welter of jollity, more jollity and gluttony. Strange how Christmas seemed to advance into October when summer had scarcely shaken off its embrace. He carefully balanced his orange juice with some limp tonic water, and from the vast window surveyed the street below.

In the distance, below the bridge, was the park where he'd sometimes cruise late Saturday evenings. On balmy summer nights, it seemed every bush shook, though not through coyness. And along from there, the dismal cavernous pub – a Santa's grotto with a fairy in every alcove. Christmas again!

The orange juice was making him bad tempered, but then he'd promised himself a much needed day on the wagon.

"Cheer up!" said a voice. "Things could be worse." Lucy was at his side, bright-eyed and odiously optimistic.

"So he cheered up…"

Joe turned round swiftly, aware of a pair of eyes behind him. The smile that greeted him was disarming. He found himself grinning back.

"And sure enough things got worse."

She pressed herself into him. She was the tactile squid of the office.

The orange juice rankled. Why didn't he just come out at work, full stop? The voice of logic prevailed. There would be the hassle, the embarrassment, the lack of a certain anonymity. In any case, was it normal to parade one's private life on one's sleeve?

Instead, he squeezed her chubby elbow, something that pleased her enormously.

"Done all your Christmas shopping then?"

Shit, Lucy! We can do better than that. I mean, look at all these wankers bustling around in stupid hats. And all this merriment is totally out of place in this cut-throat profession. I mean, after all, isn't advertising just the propagation and the proliferation of lies?

But the words never advanced beyond the ice cubes wading in the orange glass. Looking out of the window, he was aware of the pervading winter chill and the deep dissatisfaction that came with his first Twiglet.

Lucy was on to holidays. "Got anywhere planned? Me and Amy thought…"

"Dunno. I mean, I should go and see some of the long lost relatives."

"How long lost are they?"

"Ten years, I think, since I was last in touch. Laziness really. I kept meaning to write but…"

"And where are they?"

He had to think for a moment. "Sarah's in Ontario and big bro's Down Under somewhere. I'm just hopeless at writing."

"Shame on you!"

Silence, cigars, tobacco smoke.

"Don't you think they should cater for us non-smokers?" he said grumpily.

"Listen, grouch, why don't you get something better down your neck than orange juice?"

Within seconds, Lucy was proffering a glass of sparkling fizz.

"What is it?"

"Cava."

He took a long gulp. The stream of bubbles did a little to dispel the gloom.

"Just going to get something to eat," said Lucy, relinquishing him.

Joe looked at his watch, then at the frenetic festivities surrounding him. Maybe he too should snaffle something to eat, and then bugger off. The problem was that some of them were going to the Italian restaurant. He'd be expected to make up the party. Perhaps he'd just hive off to the fairy grotto instead. Bubbles tingled on his tongue. Drinking the rest of the cava, he dug deep into a sausage on a stick. He replenished his glass. Music was wheezing away in the background, anything to avoid the mask of silence – silence, the feared phenomenon. Everywhere round the city, gratuitous, ubiquitous noise, all to subdue silence, reviled like some plague. Absurd fruit machines, jangling as luminous baby rattles, in backstreet riverside pubs.

Joe turned round swiftly, aware of a pair of eyes behind him. The smile that greeted him was disarming. He found himself grinning back.

"Haven't seen you before," said Joe.

"Could be that I haven't been here before."

"The ultimate lesson in logic." Joe wondered if his remark could be construed as offensive, but his companion's eyes still smiled.

"I'm on a two-month exchange."

"Till when?"

"I'm more than halfway through. I go back the middle of January."

For a moment, Joe thought those eyes, the whole facial expression, seemed familiar.

"And how long have you been here?"

"Far too long. Far too bloody long. Far too many office parties long."

"Why don't you change it?"

The question flummoxed Joe. "Well... because..."

"You'd lose something to complain about, right?"

Again the ready grin, which put him at his ease.

"I'm Mark."

"Aloysius," said Joe, "but people here call me Lou."

"Good Catholic name," said Mark. "You haven't got an Ignatius to go with it?"

Joe ignored the flippancy, which was not unlike his own.

"And where are you from?"

"Dunedin."

Joe was trying to determine which part of Scotland it might be in, but the sweet tasting cava addled his senses.

In a moment Lucy, and possibly Emma, would be back. He could see them weaving a path through the forest of party hats.

"Look, I think there's a plan to go to a restaurant, some Italian place round the corner. I'm not much on for that, so I'm going to piss off down the pub instead."

"Sounds fine," said Mark, "do you mind if I come?"

"Sure," replied Joe, surprised.

"It's not as if I know many of the people here, and to tell you the truth, the colleagues in my department are not that friendly."

"Fine."

They got ready to go in seconds, offering no goodbyes. In the lift of spilt Fantas, crisps and cigarette ends, Joe noticed how tall Mark was. The lighted floors flashed their silhouettes through the lift grille. Funny how lifts were both so intimate and distant, he thought. Often so silent, as five or six bodies stood in uncomfortably close proximity.

In the pub he berated Mark for ordering lager.

"Don't you lot from up north drink anything else?"

"Dunno. What's the choice?" He looked puzzled as they sat down at a remote table.

"Well, plenty."

"And what's that black beer you're drinking? Treacle?"

"Winter Warmer."

"Can I try?"

As Mark leaned over to take the glass, his leg brushed against Joe's.

"It's not bad."

He kept it there till the next pint.

"Yeah, it's pretty good. I could get a liking for this. Only in winter you say?"

The Yule nectar seemed to be weaving a spell. Against the lights of the bar and the gaudy decorations, Mark's face with his dark brown eyes struck him as beautiful. His fresh cheeks and ready smile suggested an upbeat mood of optimism.

"Why don't we go back to yours?" he suggested suddenly.

"Er..." Joe was stumped for a reply. This was something new to him. The aimless cruising, the compulsive window shopping... and now, if he understood right, a decision was being expected of him.

"Yeah. Why not?"

He stood up to go, slightly swaying against the table. The pub's cacophony of raised voices receded as they stepped out into the cold night air. They spoke little, as if the singleness of purpose distracted them from all other thoughts. They walked under the bridge, which bore the weight of booming trains. By now, Lucy and Emma would be searching wayward corners, if not the loos, seeing as he had passed out there once. Then, eventually, the unruly mob would be shuffling in a disorganised serpent to the trattoria.

The train slunk slowly along the platform and they slumped into sagging late-evening seats.

"Two weeks to go. I suppose I'd better make up for lost time," Mark grinned.

"Still, it won't take you long to travel back down from Scotland."

Mark stared at him mystified. "Who said anything about Scotland? It's in New Zealand, you idiot."

"Oh, of course."

"Didn't you even notice my accent?"

They alighted from the station, passing over the empty footbridge towards the silent shops.

"Actually, it's just outside Dunedin, a place called..."

Joe stopped abruptly outside the darkened furniture shop. His thoughts were spinning round at an alarming rate, despite the hindrance of winter ale.

No wonder Mark seemed familiar.

From annual photos sent in letters that had stopped nearly eight years ago. It was just over twenty years since his elder brother had first gone out there. Standing in front of him for the first time was Mark, the nephew.

"Shit!" he shouted. "My fucking umbrella!"

"But you never had one," Mark called out anxiously.

There was a screeching of wheels. A train was heading towards the platform, going back into town. Back to the festivities, pints, trattorias, party hats.

Joe waited a moment and looked at the departing train.

As he turned round, he gazed at the tracks tapering into the night. The signals were clocked on amber.

"No one need ever know," he thought, after a long pause. "Need they?"

Spring Awakening

Slowly, under the flat, mossy stone, a pair of arms gently stirred. Small gnarled fingers stretched tentatively into the cool spring air, while an even wartier body moved clumsily from under the stone. It was a toad.

It had been a cold winter. The snow in February had given way to the rains and blustery winds of March. Frogs had quickly courted in the ponds and left. Now it was the turn of the toad.

Shuffling out of his domain, the sleepy toad felt the sun on his nose. His eyes blinked as he lay still for a moment, squatting like a piece of mud on the grass.

Then both eyes opened and the warty arms moved through the wet grass. They began to go purposefully now, but then, after these sudden exertions, the toad dived into an old hollow tree trunk and fell back to sleep.

Down in the town hall, Mr. Riley was pointing out something to his colleague, Tim.

"Every year," he said, "'undreds of them buggers get flattened. Just round 'ere."

Tim followed the knobbly finger on the map.

"So this year, to cut down the cost of clearing 'em, and it ain't pretty, we've produced this sign."

Tim looked at the prototype. A triangular piece of cardboard with the word caution and a frog-like creature above it.

"I didn't know they were dangerous, sir."

"No, you idiot," said Mr. Riley. "It's to warn the motorists, thick head!"

"Oh."

"If they drive carefully, then perhaps they won't squash so many. Then at least the dustmen won't be out all morning."

"Good idea, sir." Tim thought for a moment. "I wonder why they decided to rush all at once... to the pond, I mean."

"Wouldn't you if you'd spent ten months of the year abstaining?"

"I suppose so, sir," said Tim. "Maybe it's a bit like the January sales."

"Hmm," replied Mr. Riley doubtfully, failing to see the relevance of this remark.

The toad awoke again and this time it was a warm day. The sun began to dry the damp wood. A breeze blew and he began to scamper energetically through the long grass. His little warty legs took him instinctively and mechanically in the direction of the green, slimy pond. The damp grass brushed his tough, dry skin. Small worms and beetles appeared in his path, but today they were ignored by the otherwise rapacious mouth. His fat belly flopped onto a tuft of grass. He was still a mile or so away from the pond – the same pond, incidentally, in which, for generations, toads had congregated for their annual ritual.

For in toad folklore there is a rule that requires every toad to mate at the same pond in which he or she first sees daylight.

He was approaching the road – less than half a mile away now. He stopped, then slipped under a stile, ignoring a woozy and slumbering grass snake. His wet toes crawled onto the dry tarmac. He paused for a minute, looking carefully around him. Beyond the stile, the snake still basked.

Then, suddenly, in front of him, he saw a strange apparition. Watching him from the other side of the road was a huge toad, far bigger than any he had ever seen before. He stared at it for a moment, then again at the empty road. It was strangely deserted. Usually at this point, he crossed in convoy with a number of other toads, but then some years he'd arrived at the pond a little later than others.

He crawled closer to the toad, which was magically suspended in mid air. Then he remembered his toadhood, when he wiggled in ponds as a tiny tadpole, there had been talk, yes, of an all-powerful and all-seeing toad.

And this year, of all years, it was appearing to him! He kept very still. He looked at it, as it calmly and serenely stared back at him. He was transfixed. It seemed to be smiling at him, shining down on him. For a moment he forgot the pond, forgot everything, even a faint, distant rumble. He lowered himself before the great Toad and pressed his nose against the warm tarmac. The rumble grew.

Then, abruptly, the Toad vanished from vision and everything grew dark.

"Would you say," Mr. Riley's boss asked, "that it's been a success this year?"

"A bit hard to say," came the reply. "I suppose you can never really persuade the motorists to slow down."

"Maybe not."

"We kept finding them at odd intervals in dribs and drabs throughout the spring and summer."

"Mmm."

Mr. Riley's boss nodded sympathetically.

"I suppose what it needs is a few more signs."

Soft Touch

I hate Mondays, just as I hate all days. But particularly this day, because I know it's all starting again. Five days of it. Five! Could be like a month sometimes, when I look at it from the waning security of Sundays.

As I put down my trowel, a great, long, slithering globule trickles down my neck, my blouse, and I look up anxiously to see if it's a passing bird, but no, it's just a giant spot of rain. Clouds are gathering on the horizon and all because I thought of Monday.

Over near the park, Mr. Burns is walking his dog and I nod to him from the sanctum of my garden, as his overweight spaniel sideshuffles, like himself, past the telephone box.

"Nice evening. Looks like rain, though."

"Yes," I say, putting down my trowel.

After our routine exchange, I step into the still-red telephone box. There's a smell of pee and ash and sometimes cashew nuts. I call this cocktail 'panache', the very thing that's missing... A click. "Yes, hello Myra. Yes... yes. Maybe you'd like to come next Sunday. I thought... Oh, you can't. Oh well... No, never mind. No, no. Oh, the money's running out. Hang on. Yes, I've got another one. Yes... No. No, I don't think you can on this box. They've changed it."

I put the phone down. I always phone Myra from a public phone box, because she talks too much. Spends half her life on the phone. And yet she never comes – to visit that is – because she's permanently perched on the wires between Bristol and Birmingham and Macclesfield and...

Can't say I didn't try. I take the long walk back, ruminating over Myra's words. Past the green, the church; lights on in the adjoining hall. Tea and coffee and iced cakes, and its chiming clock makes time draw nearer. It's seven o'clock by the church tower clock, and flickering TV sets show Songs of Praise or Stars on Sunday. The congregation of three leave the church, looking across the green as if uncertain which way to go. But there are no stars on Sunday, for behind the faintly glowing street lamps, the darkness stretches into Monday, Tuesday and beyond.

I'm having a boiled egg now. The walk round the green tired me out. And I remember the time when they said you should go to work on an egg. And we all laughed and said that's a funny form of transport. I'm sure it's more reliable, though, than those new slab-sided buses with no conductors and concertina doors. Mrs. Webb was stuck in them the other week and it took them an hour to get them open again. That's progress, but I'm slicing my egg and thinking of the little boy on the advert. Auntie, I wonder what's become of him, for it was Auntie who was the provider of the boiled egg.

I clear the plates and am now in front of the mirror. I don't like that face much, so I'll paint it up. Good and proper; redecorate. No wonder they call it war paint, for so many of us have to do battle. If Jim were here now, my fights would be over. I could tell him. He'd listen. So many of them don't now. I can feel his hands on my shoulders before he'd hug me, kiss me, run for his bus. He ran too fast one day and... You see, that's why...

The wind's blowing up as I step outside. Momentarily, I bow into it and my eyes are covered with dust; my newly painted eyes, as I scurry towards the stop. Going past me, Mr. Jones in his bright red car. But he never stops to give a lift. Doesn't think like that. Doesn't think. His car, his terrain, his jam jar. A foreign bottom crumpling the seats. Unthinkable. No, they don't think. I've noticed that. We're all too busy looking at the cracks in the pavement to notice each other.

I'm holding up the bus this morning because I can't find the right pass. The driver waits and holds me to ransom as I, in turn, hold them in the serenade of sighs and tutting. But all's well and we're on the move, carrying on into deepest, darkest Monday.

Outside the Corn Exchange, which will soon re-house the TV company, I get out and walk up the rained-on street. The building, the office, the turnstile gates, the security man brooding at his desk, the voiceless nod, the lift, the view from parapet and balcony.

He's not in yet and I breathe a sigh of relief. One Monday, the curtain-raiser lasted all day, and he didn't come in. By three, I knew I was in for a reprieve; suspense over as the wife rang in. Conference lasted another day, apparently. Henry too busy to phone me. Could I see to...? For a moment I was listening to the doubt in her voice. I didn't say much. Her light, bright warble betraying...

I sit down carefully at my desk and slowly sift through the Classified Section, as I always do when he's not here. Daydreaming, I know, and as Myra says, not too many things going for you when you reach a certain time in life. Myra, halfway down the line to Birmingham; spirit of optimism and hope.

The lift whirrs. He's here. Outside. Outside the glass panels. Then there's a tap. A knock. No, not him. With him the door opens and a chill wind blows into the office.

"Could you sign here, please?" The delivery boy holds out a pen, despite my formidable armoury. For a moment, I thought he said "miss" and I'm wondering in what way I manage to look a miss. But he repeats, "No, here please," and points a finger that almost touches mine. Contact of the welcome kind and his eyes, dark and serious, give the flicker of a smile.

Eleven now. Eleven. The lift whirrs. Someone gets out. The breeze, the familiar step. It's him.

"Good morning, Ann."

"Good morning, Mr. Lawrence."

His immaculate suit and toothpaste stripes, sunken piggy eyes – not like the delivery boy's – and flabby, wobbling cheeks. From his lips there are traces of saliva, which draw my eyes to them, and that sudden recollection of horror, when, after one long liquid lunch, he pressed them slobbering into mine. For one week after, I was the recipient of presents.

He has to touch, you see. Just as he touches everything that's female. Assembled objects on a mantelpiece of life. It's as if he's taking stock.

I wait for the errant hand to touch my shoulder, as he leans over to cast an eye on the state of my written competence. The hand will linger while he asks me anything; banalities, what I did on… Questions whose answers are never listened to. The solution, I've found, is to keep the talk as brief as possible, in the hope that the molesting fingers will go away. Monosyllables, however, are no use. They bring on the souciant charm.

"Everything okay? Sure?"

The hand squeezes my shoulder tighter, so that behind my inward shaking, I give empty. hollow answers.

"Had a good weekend?" as my eyes mist over the month's statistics.

Then, suddenly, my fingers are in revolt. The hand is between my neck and shoulders. The thick, glass ashtray is light and pliable as a rubber ring. It sways and leaps into my hand. I jump up.

It only takes a few seconds but there's blood now, sliding down his face, like the cracked shell of a hard-boiled egg. Little streams. The fingers that were massaging my neck crumple and like a collapsible balloon, he's stretched out on the floor. He's motionless, apart from the air hissing from his mouth. There's a silence in the office. A relentless ticking of the clock.

"Yes, I had a good weekend," I say, as the fingers move further up and down, rubbing the shiny chain which hangs loosely, limply round my neck.

Ebb Tide

She glanced up at the clock. She had better be ready, she thought, seeing as they were coming at two. And Quentin was always on time; punctual to a tee. How dark it was in this room; it needed some colour, some brightening up, just like those dreary clothes that nestled together in the wardrobe. She had parted company with them years ago, but for some reason they had never quite made it to the charity shop.

There was a sudden burst of music outside; a sad little tune clattering beyond the window. Ella remembered it was the ice cream van. Like the Pied Piper of Hamlyn, it suddenly brought children out of the dormant houses that flanked the green. From her window, the view was full of colours, as excited reds and stripy yellows jostled impatiently in the queue. But no ice creams had ever passed her lips. The van sang again as it continued its journey and the colours disappeared.

Through the glass in the front door, she could see a shape approaching and imagined they were coming for her already. But no, the shape was much too squat for Quentin.

Quentin. Why had they chosen that name? It seemed so arid and dry now. So academic and scholarly.

The shape bowed a little and inserted its hand towards the letterbox. A white card came tumbling onto the mat and in a second she was scrambling to pick it up. The card said simply, J. B. Dennis, specialist in double-glazing. Ella shuddered. Why double it when one pane was enough? And she consigned J.B. to the pedal-bin, to lie on top of takeaways and pizzas.

She was wading now, wading through water, soft and shallow, not cold, and, for a moment, she could see the sun behind the pier.

The railway, suspended above and perching on its wooden slats, glinted in the light; a green and white train on a journey to nowhere. The water sparkled and there was the slight hint of a breeze. The sand and mud were forming intricate patterns like the webbed feet of gulls, as the relentless tide ebbed, drifted, far into the wide estuary and beyond the oil refinery; now all but vanishing, leaving her to tread a silent desert with only the company of the pier and the barnacled sewage pipe, the discovery of which had put her permanently off cockles and whelks. There was a smell of fish now, not jellied eels or mussels, as her soft slippers squelched onto lino.

"Stupid! Stupid!" she cried. She was paddling across the kitchen floor, where no trains ran, looking at the gaping door of the rapidly thawing freezer. Somehow she'd switched it off and left the door ajar. The concealed icebergs had unleashed their flood; a microcosm of the world outside.

Quickly, she set to work, spreading redundant copies of the Local Advertiser and Estate Agent Weekly across the kitchen floor. They drank greedily, detached bungalows absorbing copious amounts of stale water, turning beige in the process as the kitchen reverted to its coastal scene.

They mustn't see this, she thought, fetching a brittle mop. They'd soon be here and this would provide the undeniable proof with which Lorna and Quentin would seal their smug triumph. More copies, quickly, more Advertisers and more soggy rows of houses. Ella flung the mop back in the bucket, then gathered up the limp squares of newspaper, opening the back door in the hope that the fishy smell would leave.

"Colours!" she said out loud, remembering her earlier chain of thought before the kitchen had turned into a seaside resort. That was it! Something to brighten the place, liven it up a bit, instead of its funereal gloom.

Beyond the hedges, the ice cream van tinkled faintly, very faintly, in the distance. Why had she never tried one? She was trying to remember. And today would have been her last chance. Looking out of the window, the green lay unpeopled and empty.

Ever since the new people had come, the ones with money, you hardly saw anyone. Occasionally, you saw them driving away under their canopies of steel or their oversized jeeps.

Still they had not yet come.

Quentin. She had never really liked him, unlike George whom she never saw. There was something too neat and clean about him. He had never looked lived in; a sort of walking clinic; a bland and dreary clerk, and yet he was greatly admired for his efficiency, his diligence. To Ella, however, he was just a walking suit in grey. Grey. Yes. And yet he must have had a personality once, sometime, before he set his foot upon the working ladder. And the wife! Lorna. What did he see in her or she in him? Lorna with the smile that always drooped downwards, just the briefest elevation of a permanently downturned mouth.

Lorna, the sound of a grey afternoon in winter…

The last soggy square was stuffed into the pedal bin, groaning as she released it, a gaping mouth as big as a basking crocodile or a church flower lady's. She stopped. Flowers. Of course. That would brighten the place up. What time was it? She could get some from across the way, from Mr. Cuthwade, the helpful vegetable gardener. Some lilies, or gentian even. That would be nice. She liked the blousy smell of lilies.

Suddenly, an urgent bleating filled the room. Thinking of runaway sheep, she picked up the receiver, but the slippery eel fell from her grasp. Ella reached for it once again; a difficult balancing act.

"Yes." She was having to reassure the anxious voice at the other end. "I'm fine. No, really I am. Of course. It was the phone. I dropped it on the beach."

Silence. Puzzled silence. She could hear it making quick calculations. What had she done? What had she said? She'd said that word. Said it. Too late. Far too late to recover it; sweep up the damage. The broken vase of indiscretion lay in fragments across the floor. What was she thinking of? And what were they thinking? It was further proof that she wasn't up to it. Couldn't cope. And so, therefore, the move. How could she recover the word 'beach'? Bleach? That would be even worse. Peach?

"I dropped the phone. My hands were wet," she lied. "Yes, I'm fine. Just tidying up. No, don't worry about anything."

"We'll be around shortly," he had said. The downcast smile and the squeaky clean suit were coming for her. Off to kidnap her and ensconce her in the purpose-built granny flat. A life sentence, and she wasn't even a granny. She went once again to the window. A last taste of freedom and goodbye to the coloured shapes that sometimes danced on the green. Goodbye to the Pied Piper and his one tune. Colours, she remembered again. Colours, and she sat down for a moment, out of breath, and as she did so, one final colour began to take shape as she slowly removed her clothes.

When, at a little after two, in a rare lapse of punctuality, the promised visitors appeared at the door, they experienced a lengthier wait than usual.

"I told you, you should have brought the key. I mean…"

"She likes to feel it's still her…" Quentin's words were blown away by Lorna's irritation. They looked at each other, then talked again about the phone and the nonsensical 'beach' incident. What had been going on?

Eventually, the door swung open to a pair of impatient frowns. As Lorna glanced up, she let out a piercing scream. Quentin took her arm. Confronting them was a barely recognisable figure; one that looked back sweetly and demurely and, at the same time, smugly.

"Good grief!" cried Quentin.

The genial apparition had emerged as if from a dark lagoon. Creating a rich cocktail of mud from the garden, from a soil that was as dark as it was fertile, she had daubed herself extravagantly from head to foot. The vaguely Polynesian grass skirt added a touch of coquettishness.

"Come in, dear," she said to Quentin, ignoring Lorna and treading over the kitchen floor that had once been Southend-on-Sea. "I'll just make us a nice cup of tea."

The onlookers gazed speechless. She put the kettle on. "You would like one before we go, wouldn't you? And then whenever you're ready. There's no hurry."

Poetic Licence

There were times when she had come close to strangling her, throttling her, garrotting her! When Doris announced she was coming on the October weekend too, Mildred could happily have done all three.

"It's a writing weekend, dear," she said. "And you're not a writer."

She hesitated for a moment, fearing that some long-lost forsaken manuscript had been concealed from her in an empty drawer or chamber pot, and now awaited a chorus of approbation. This, fortunately, was not Doris's line of approach.

"It says you can bring guests," she mumbled, pointing to the leaflet in which a neo-timber-boarded hotel squatted over a babbling stream.

"Oh yes, so it does." Mildred remembered, cursing Mr. Pughsley's agitation for change at their last annual meeting. "You'd be bored silly," she soothed. "Really."

"Why?" Doris countered. "What makes you think that? And why go if you're bored? I mean, how do you know I'll be bored, especially when you're always telling me how good the stuff is they keep churning out?"

Mildred was about to impale her sister-in-law on an imaginary railing, but instead conceded defeat. Ever since Harry had gone to the eternal snooker room in the sky, she had promised that she would look after Doris and keep in touch with Kitty.

Kitty had proved no problem, and was even rumoured to be having what was termed a meaningful relationship with her postman, which was what caused Doris to descend on her.

"It's no good," she confided. "I'm in the way. I know it. And when I'm not, they keep going off to endless stamp exhibitions."

Her long weekend of being an 'evacuee' had slithered now into months and soon it was clear to 'Mildy', as 'Dor' invariably called her, that Doris was not going back.

At first it hadn't been too bad. Mildy retreated more frequently to the allotment club that met every Sunday afternoon, until Doris suddenly announced that she too had acquired an interest in gardening. That was when the first homicidal flicker involving a large pair of garden shears had taken place. Instead, Mildred had diverted her frustrations on the sunken privet hedge behind the lily pond, and indulged in an unusual display of topiary. But now the writing weekend! That was really the last straw!

The taxi slid into the station car park, a funereal bead against an early autumn sky.

"Do they always talk that much on the trains?" Doris grumbled. "Thank you for this, thank you for that. There was a packet of crisps on the line, so we'll be delayed for..."

"Always," answered Mildred, who remembered that on Spanish trains they played flamenco music, and shuddered involuntarily.

"Those cows," said Doris, gesturing out of the taxi window. "There's something wrong with them."

"They're Saddlebacks, "Mildred replied. "They're meant to look like that."

At the hotel entrance, Mildred was fervently hoping that Doris would find fault with something, but now she was moving into enthused vein.

Down the hotel steps tripped Mr. Henry Pughsley in welcoming mode.

"Mildred, this must be the lovely sister-in-law you've told me about."

For a moment, Mildred was confused and looked around. Kitty, it must have been Kitty she'd told him about. But Doris... lovely?

"Welcome," he beamed, leaning forward to kiss Doris's outstretched hand.

She gave a kittenish nod of approval.

"He's got a partner," Mildred intoned later into her ear. "A retired librarian from Southsea."

Undaunted, the smile of eagerness still spread across her companion's face.

"Called George."

The smile dipped a little, then vanished rather like an expiring light bulb.

"You didn't tell me it was full of nancies."

"You never asked, dear."

That evening Mr. Pughsley was dispensing the 'batting order' for the following day. "

"He gathers the subjects up and arranges who reads when," Mildred whispered, anticipating Doris's interruption of curiosity, but her 'sister' was more interested in watching a grey heron paddling in the stream beyond the window.

It was when the meeting came to an end that consternation finally broke loose. Mr. Pughsley's bell, which was occasionally rung to silence the out of control ladies, had gone missing.

"I put it on the table when I came in," he wailed in agitation. "George bought it in Takoradi."

"Help us look for it, Doris," said Mildred, but instead she was addressing an empty chair, as the resident cuckoo was now walking briskly across the car park.

They searched well up to dinner, having little time to digest the sherry, and as they chewed forlornly over appropriately named minute steaks, it seemed a cloud had fallen over the assembly. Miss Albuquerque helped Mr. Pughsley to his room. What was to become of them all? Without the means to silence the riotous ladies – although occasionally there was one token gentleman – only anarchy would prevail.

"Everyone's gone to bed early," Mildred moaned. "Very early. And all because of that missing bell."

"Bell," said Doris. "What bell?"

"Mr. Pughsley's instant rapier," replied Mildred. "He's very upset."

"Was it a little white china thing with a naked limbo dancer on the inside?"

Mildred was looking in horror at Doris. "You didn't!" she cried. "You've broken it!"

"Nothing of the sort," Doris replied. "I took it to reception. I thought it had got mislaid."

An instant vision of a room reduced to chaos, of various rheumatic knees crawling under tables, of cloths being carefully unwrapped leapt into her mind. And all for nothing. She knew Doris should never have come, knew it would be no good. But then, as she reflected, it was Henry's suggestion, after all, to bring along guests this year for their biggest and farewell bash.

"Why did you have to interfere?" she snapped. "They're probably searching half of Hertfordshire by now, and there it is lying in reception."

Doris was in no way contrite. "Well, if that's the thanks I get for trying to help, for being a responsible citizen, for wanting to play my part, then I'm off to bed. Sort yourself out!"

At that very moment, Mildred thought she heard a far-away waft of the Hallelujah Chorus, but when she stepped down into the bar ten minutes later, they were playing Georgie Fame. Oona Pookenberger, actress and radio star, who'd once made a guest appearance in The Archers, was sitting in front of her gin and tonic.

"Say, wasn't that bell thing a no-no? Everyone's gone to bed. Who could have run off with it? Have you written your story yet?"

"Oh yes," Mildred smiled, at the same time rummaging in her handbag. It was not until the third and final rummage was complete and she sat down again, listening to the ample cushion sigh beneath her, that the awful realisation set in. She was one story light. Had brought only one instead of the customary two.

The bubbles on Oona's drink looked flat.

"I'm off to write mine," Oona confessed. "You know me. It's usually a four in the morning job. Then I'm so knackered, I have to pinch myself to keep awake in the stories."

She downed the rest of her drink. "Goo' night, honey."

"Good night," said Mildred. She sat in glum realisation. Doris. It was Doris. She'd been so distracted by her coming on the weekend, that she'd forgotten her story entitled 'Kiki the Parakeet'. It was probably lying on the bedside table, pages curling up in the dry, residual heat of the bedroom, waiting for the audience it craved. But it was not to be.

"Would madame like e-something to drink?" A voice of consolation cooed in her ear. She looked up to see the red and white liveried barman collecting the empties. For a moment she was falling into those dark eyes, tumbling into a bottomless well...

"Yes, I would," she said.

"Yes, madame," he said, in a voice that was both attentive and subservient.

"What is your wish?"

Well you, actually, thought Mildred, but instead was mouthing the platitudes, "A sherry and... where are you from?"

"Barcelona."

"What's your name?" before he had even time to finish.

"Javier," he spluttered, "but no one can manage that name here, so when I work in Bakingstoke, they call me Darren."

"Cheers, Darren," said Mildred, feeling like she could run round the park. "And have one yourself too."

It occurred to her afterwards that Darren may have misheard 'have one' for 'have fun', but as he was showing her the carpets in the servants' quarters after the bar closed, she was hardly going to complain.

As she crept smugly from his room at around four in the morning, she thought she could see a light on under Doris's door. Had she been waiting up?

Deftly, to avoid detection, she slunk silently across the carpets and clicked the door to. She would celebrate by drinking the contents of her mini-bar. But first, the matter for which she had come. The story.

Pen was gliding swiftly across paper. Inspired by Darren and his cocktail shaker, words flowed, poured even, and very faintly, in the distance, she thought she could hear the rhythmic tapping of Oona's typewriter.

The next morning, she staggered in to breakfast. Feeling some affinity with the scrambled egg that lay splattered on vast oval plates, she thought back with grateful weariness to the nocturnal antics. Two bursts of creativity. She had never done it before, as she smiled quietly to herself, whilst avoiding Doris's questioning gaze.

"I knocked on your door."

"I was writing my story."

But Doris continued to stare disbelievingly at Mildred's wrecked appearance.

"Finished it?"

"Oh yes," Mildred nodded.

As usual, that lunchtime, they were across the road in the pub, looking wistfully at the jugged hare casserole that would sabotage and confuse appetites for the hotel evening meal.

"Did you finish your story?" Oona P. asked.

"Yes," said Mildred.

"I'm doing my second one tonight. By the way, where's your sister?"

"That's a point," said Mildred, who had happily forgotten her. Perhaps the thought of having to buy a drink had left her languishing in the sanctuary of the hotel.

It was during the prawn salad that Mildred, anticipating an attack of wind, declined a second drink and slipped back across the road to the hotel. Feeling mildly guilty as she passed the hotel reception with beery breath, she looked in at the bar. Alas, no Darren as yet, and no Doris either.

She ascended the staircase and took out the absurdly large room key. The bed was made up, the pillaged contents of the fridge shipped away, and there, to one side, was a note on the table. It was then that Mildred turned half-anxiously to the new manuscript perched on a bedside chair.

'I read your story,' Doris had written, 'and I was incensed. I know of course that literature acts as some kind of confession, but if that's the sort of thing that happens on your weekends, then I wish to have no further association with it. You should be ashamed of yourself. At your age! And with a Spaniard too!'

Catalan, actually, thought Mildred, in a pedantic moment that would have done Doris proud.

'I've decided I'm going to move back home rather than run the risk of being resident in a brothel. In fact, I shall probably contact St. Martin's Convent and enquire about late vocations. Yours, in great disapproval, Doris'.

This time, the room took on a golden glow. The writing weekend had worked like none other. She would buy Mr. Pughsley a stack of handbells. She could hug him! She would make over half her house to Darren, who wanted to give her Spanish lessons. And she would write all her stories well into the night now.

All this, she thought, while in the distance, building up to a giant crescendo, came a massive Hallelujah chorus.